THE SEA TURTLE DID IT

THE
SEA TURTLE
DID
IT

KAY DEW SHOSTAK

THE SEA TURTLE DID IT
Copyright © 2020 by Kay Dew Shostak.
All rights reserved.

This book is a work of fiction. The characters, incidents, and dialogue are drawn from the author's imagination and are not to be construed as real. Any resemblance to actual events or persons, living or dead, is entirely coincidental.

Printed in the United States of America. No part of this book may be used or reproduced in any manner whatsoever without written permission except in the case of brief quotations embodied in articles and reviews.

ISBN: 978-1-7350991-0-1

SOUTHERN FICTION: Cozy Mystery / Southern Mystery / Florida Mystery / Island Mystery / Empty Nest Mystery / Clean Mystery / Small Town Mystery

Text Layout and Cover Design by Roseanna White Designs
Cover Images from www.Shutterstock.com

Author photo by Susan Eason with www.EasonGallery.com

Published by August South Publishing. You may contact the publisher at:
AugustSouthPublisher@gmail.com

Dedicated to Mary Duffy of the Amelia Island Sea Turtle Watch who answered my questions. Any mistakes I made are despite her sharing her wonderful store of knowledge. She and all the Turtle Watch volunteers are one major reason Amelia Island is the wonderful place it is!

*And as always,
To our home –
Amelia Island and Fernandina Beach*

*While Sophia Island and Sophia Beach are based on you,
the characters and situations can only be found in my imagination.
Oh, and in my books.*

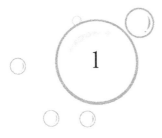

1

"But it's not turtle season," my friend Tamela exclaims.

Again.

We are walking, practically running, along the beach, not even pretending to appreciate this glorious April morning because, well, apparently the world is ending. Around us others are walking and running in the same direction. I shorten my stride to keep Tamela from having to huff while she talks. My legs are a bit longer than hers, and why should I hurry anyway? I'm not even sure what the hurry is all about.

My short friend grabs onto my forearm, then raises her other hand to point ahead of us at the growing crowd up near the dunes.

"See? There it is. Oh my word! Jewel, is that the police?" Tamela's hold on my arm tightens, and she moans as her shoulders drop.

She catches her breath as I point to men in yellow coats arriving from over the dunes. "Looks like Sophia Island's fire department is here too. I still don't understand what the big deal is. I thought protecting turtles coming on shore was a good thing." My husband and I being newcomers to this island off the Atlantic coast of North Florida means we are behind on a lot things. Today, apparently, it is turtle habits.

As we reach the outskirts of the crowd, Tamela plunges ahead, still holding my arm. When she suddenly stops, I bump into her. She drops my arm to hold her hand over her mouth. She's moaning again and shaking her head.

Over her shaking head, I see a large mound of sand. Its circumference is staked out with a broken beach chair, driftwood, and garbage that looks like it came from the nearby garbage can. Pieces of broken Styrofoam cooler are buried standing up to help form a barrier protecting the dome of sand. There's even some beer bottles buried upside down around the edges. Tying all this together is what looks like old kite string. It's circled around and around, tying the site up pretty well.

I don't get it. It looks to me like the person did a good job of marking the place and protecting it. That's the idea, right? Protecting the nest of turtle eggs? I bend down to say this to Tamela just as the policeman walks closer, and I notice our friend Lucy is right by his side.

Lucy Fellows is a mover and shaker on Sophia Island. She works at city hall, is on a ton of committees, plays tennis with anyone who is anyone, and, most important of all, she's a native, born and raised right here. She looks crisp, but a Florida crisp. We've always lived up north, and it's taken some getting used to Florida's casual dress code. It's almost like the more important a person is on Sophia Island, the more laidback they're dressed. Today Lucy has on khaki capris, a Sophia Island golf shirt, and flip-flops. Now, I've found some of these flip-flops are really expensive. We're not talking the $1.99 ones I grew up with, although I've seen lots of those at Annie's church too. She's dragged me there a couple times, and I kind of like it.

Lucy looks up and scans the crowd, and then her eyes alight on Tamela. She points at Tamela and crooks her finger for her to come over. Tamela grabs my arm again and drags me alongside the turtle nest with her.

Lucy pulls Tamela into a hug, then me as well. Hugging is another thing I've had to get used to since moving here. It's apparently really big in the South.

"Oh, Lucy, isn't this just awful?" Tamela says. "What should we do?"

The police officer steps out from behind Lucy. "Good morning, Ms. Stout. Ms. Mantelle."

"Good morning, Officer Bryant." We all met a couple of months ago when my husband's cousin died—okay, was murdered by his mother. Yuck. Doesn't that sound awful? Anyway, Officer Bryant is the son of another friend, Annie. Speaking of whom, I'm surprised she's not here.

Officer Bryant turns to Tamela. "Ms. Stout, Ms. Fellows here says you might have some supplies for officially marking a nest since you're one of the Turtle Trackers? Do you happen to have some in your car?"

Tamela moans again, making me really wonder what the big deal is with these turtles. I try to catch Lucy's eye to share a laugh at her hysterics, but Lucy looks just as serious. "It's not turtle season," Tamela says. "I haven't put everything in my car yet. I can call my husband to bring it, though. We only live a few blocks away." She pulls out her phone, but Officer Bryant puts his hand out.

"That's okay. We have some on the way. Nobody is prepared quite this early in the year to mark a nest."

Lucy folds her arms and harrumphs. "Because it's not a turtle nest." She's angry. She's not the only angry one, I realize, now that I look around at the faces in the crowd. Lucy's voice rises. "Not only is it too early, there are no tracks. No tracks at all, and the mound is too high, too big overall. Someone is playing a trick! It's absolutely not a nest and should not be marked as one. We should do away with all this garbage and level it."

"Over my dead body!" a darkly tanned woman on the other side of the crowd exclaims. "Maybe this poor mother was confused or the tides washed her here. We owe it to her to protect her babies as if they were our very own!" The woman steps up to the edge of the circle of debris and waves her arm at the slapdash beer bottle/cooler/beach chair protection. "Someone went to such trouble to protect this nest, and I will defend it with my very life."

"Don't be so dramatic, Sheila," Lucy says with a roll of her eyes, Tamela's tragic moans apparently forgotten. "You don't even know what you're talking about!" She then bows her head and mumbles at us, "That's why she is *never* getting into our group."

Lucy turns her back on the nest and the crowd and talks quietly with Officer Bryant, so quietly that Tamela and I can't hear what they are saying. We turn our attention to the woman still lamenting the poor turtle babies she's ready to lay down her life for, but she's saying nothing new. Tamela and I shrug at each other. Then, just as Lucy and Officer Bryant turn back around, one of the firefighters comes trudging across the beach-access walkway. "I've got the stakes and tape," he shouts. "Everyone move back!"

In one arm he's carrying a half-dozen wooden stakes, the kind used for yard signs. In his other hand is a roll of yellow plastic streamer with the word 'Caution' emblazoned in bold, black print.

He receives applause and a few whoops from the crowd. Lucy's face becomes stonier as he advances. "There are rules we should be following," she says, but she's drowned out as everyone is pushed back by Sheila and the firefighters. I notice the firefighters are not looking at Lucy. When one of them does, he grimaces at her and says, "Sorry, Ms. Fellows.

Chief says we gotta err on the side of caution."

Out of the side of her mouth she says, "Oh, I just bet he did." She takes a deep breath. "No worries, Chip. It's not your fault that your boss has gone over to the dark side. You'd never know he was born and raised here by the way he chases after the tourists and newcomers like a puppy looking for a belly rub!"

Sheila has made her way to our side, and she huffs. "Maybe we newcomers care more about this island because we appreciate just how special it is. You natives want us to go away so you don't ever have to change, much less learn about where you live!"

Officer Bryant steps in between the two women. Lucy looks like she's aiming to ignore him, to plow right over him, so I put my arm out and pull her toward me. She flings around like she's going to hit someone, but then she sees me and stops short.

I nudge her away. "Let's walk down to the water, Lucy. They're going to do what they feel they need to. They aren't doing it just because that other woman wants them to. She didn't win. She's just, I guess, on the right side of being careful this time."

While I talk, I walk, and Lucy lets me

guide her. When we clear the crowd, she takes another deep breath and strides ahead of me to stand where the waves are breaking against the sand. The early sun has turned the water's surface to diamonds, and each crest shines with an unnatural whiteness. The breeze is cool, and the salt water smells fresh and cold.

"See? It's not warm enough for there to have been a turtle laying eggs here." She swipes her arm to her side. "Do you see any tracks? No. None."

Tamela catches up with us and walks close to Lucy's other side. "Ignore that Sheila woman. You know she's just an old-fashioned bully. There's one on every playground, and as a retired teacher, I know it's best to just ignore them. Isn't that right, Jewel?"

I nod as we angle off to walk along the water. "You know her?" I ask. "You said something about not letting her in your group. The turtle group?"

Lucy screws up her mouth, then looks up at me with her blue eyes squinted. "Yeah, Turtle Trackers. I shouldn't have said that, but she just came around trying to be the boss. She doesn't want to be a substitute, which is how all of our new volunteers start. She wants her own territory to patrol, and she wants it now. She also only wants the area outside her house, but that's, well, that's already taken."

"So, when do the turtles usually start nesting?" I ask.

"May. Possibly the end of April, but not when we've had such a cold spring. But there are no tracks—and that huge mound! Someone is playing a practical joke, and guess what? It's not funny! Wait till the FWNC"—she answers my question before it can get out—"the Florida Wildlife and Nature Conservancy gets involved. They'll track down who did this. I called them first thing. You can't count on the local officials, as they are completely swayed by the tourism board."

We walk for a minute before I say what I'm thinking. "So if there's really not a nest, what does it matter if it gets marked? I mean, nothing will happen, right?"

Tamela meets my eyes and shrugs. She's lived here a while but only joined the turtle group when she retired. I believe she said she's still a sub.

Lucy sighs. She stops and turns to look back at the crowd still surrounding the possible nest. "It's just we worked so hard for so long to get people to take us seriously. I don't like being made fun of. We are a serious group with an important mission."

We watch the crowd for a bit, then walk back in their direction. The closer we get, the louder that woman Sheila gets. She's giving a lesson on North Florida turtle nesting habits for all to hear. She's wearing slouchy pants and a sweatshirt with the sleeves cut off. She's large, but I think it's mostly muscle. Her hair is in a ponytail, and in her vehemence it's jumping around from side to side. Her preaching has some in the crowd echoing her and amen-ing like they're in church.

I can't help but grin. As I nudge Lucy I say, "Plus, you really don't like that woman."

Lucy scowls, but then her shoulders relax and she smiles. "Yeah, there is that."

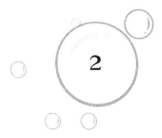

2

"Can you believe I had a doctor's appointment when all this happened this morning?" Annie says. She sashays toward the rear of Coffee Sophia, blowing past the line of people waiting for their late morning pick-me-up. "My phone was blowing up, and there I was in my all-together waiting for Doctor Zhivago. Liked to kill me lying there wondering what in the world was happening." She plops down at the last table, her arm full of bangle bracelets rattling.

"Wait, what?" I ask as I sit too. "Your doctor's name is Zhivago? Like the movie?"

"No, silly. He's Russian. Can't say his name. I bet Lucy was fit to be tied. Tell me—"

"No, one more. You were all together in what?"

She settles back in her chair, and I can see her moving back through our conversation. "Oh, in my all-together." She leans forward and whispers, "I was naked. Well, under that flimsy paper gown. Anyway, he's a women's doctor. That's why I couldn't get my phone or even just hightail it out of there."

"Oh. Okay. Never mind, sorry." She doesn't seem to be embarrassed, but my face is hot. I look around to get off the subject. "It doesn't seem right for us to just sit here and have them bring us our drinks when everyone else is standing around waiting."

Annie shrugs. "Eden likes waiting on me and my friends. Besides, she has a favor to ask you."

"Me? What could Eden possibly want to ask me?"

"Just wait. She'll be out in a minute. Let me answer this text." Annie bends over her phone, her fingers flying. Annie is a widow with six grown children who all live and work on Sophia Island. The officer this morning, Aiden Bryant, is her son, and his girlfriend works here at Coffee Sophia. Her name is Eden, and she's really sweet. At first I found all her tattoos distracting, but apparently her parents own a tattoo parlor, so it makes sense that she'd have plenty. I met her right after we moved here, when we were trying to clear my husband, Craig, of his cousin's murder. Eden gets lots of information from Aiden about what the police are doing, information Aiden would never share with his mother. Annie and my other friends pretty much solved the murder. I was in the middle of it, too, but it was all I could do to keep track of everybody's name.

Craig, of course, was innocent. Okay, well, he was innocent of murder, but he was completely guilty of not telling the truth about several things. Mainly, that the huge, decrepit old house we inherited from his aunt Corabelle Mantelle came with strings attached and that we can't sell it for five years. Craig dealt with (read: ignored) that news by not retiring as planned and completely blindsiding me with a work project in south Florida. Leaving me here alone.

But, for the first time in my adult life, at least I've made some real friends.

"Here you go!" Eden says as she swoops toward our table. "Vanilla latte for Miss Jewel and mint for Miss Annie." As she sets the big ceramic cups and saucers on the table, she eases into a chair, half sitting on one bent leg. "I'm taking my break so we can talk." She turns to Annie. "Did you tell her?"

Annie shakes her head and lifts her cup. "Nope."

The young woman turns her whole body toward me. She's slight with short, choppy red hair that gives her a pixie look. Her tattoos lean heavily on the plant and floral variety. One flower on her cheek colors when she blushes, and it's actually quite charming. "Miss Jewel. I have a proposal for you. My parents are moving their shop downtown, and the building has an apartment upstairs where they are going to live." She lays a hand on the table. "That means I need to find a place to live since they're selling our house."

"Okay," I say. "But you are staying in the area, aren't you?"

"I want to, but prices are pretty high here, you know, especially on the island. So I was thinking, well, you know how I was going to come look at some of your furniture? Help you with figuring out if anything is worth anything?"

"Yes! I can't believe I haven't had you over yet. I'd practically forgotten that you know about that kind of thing."

"Well," she says, a bit shyly, "what if I move in with you? I can pay some, but then I'd also work helping you with the furniture and the other antiques. I could also clean or paint. Whatever you need!"

I lean back in my chair. "Live in our house? With Craig and me?"

Annie motions with her eyes for Eden to be quiet; then my friend with her shiny, silver curls folds her arms on the table and leans her ample bosom over them. "Jewel. When's the last time Craig actually came home for a weekend?"

I splutter. "Well, he was going to come home for Easter last weekend."

"Did he?"

"Things got hectic and, well, no." I settle my hands in my lap and look down at them.

Eden gets up. "No hurry at all," she says. "And no pressure either. Right, Miss Annie?" She looks at Annie and then turns to smile at me. "You just think about it. I've gotta get back to work." She dashes off, and I glare at Annie.

"That was so awkward. Why didn't you tell me what she wanted?"

"I didn't want to forewarn you. I was actually hoping you'd be too embarrassed to say no. I told Eden to not get all flibbertigibbet and leave without an answer. Of course she did anyway. You think stuff to death! This would be good for you. You like young people, and you're completely stuck on what to do with that mausoleum you got hung around your neck." Annie huffs and throws up her arms. "Lord knows I've tried to get in there and help you move forward, or backward, or up. Just move! You need Eden, and she needs you. At least try it. Give it a month. What do you have to lose?"

Eden comes out of the back. I see her glance in our direction, then look away as she rushes past us.

"Tomorrow," I blurt to Annie. "I'll talk to Craig tonight, and I'll make a decision by tomorrow. Okay?"

Annie rolls her big, purply eyes. "Fine. I'll take what I can get. Now drink up. Lucy just texted me. FWCNN—no, that's not right, whatever—the wildlife nature group is going to be at the beach in thirty minutes. I want to see this supposed turtle nest myself. The pictures on Facebook and Twitter make it look way too big to be a turtle nest."

"Are you in the Turtle Tracker group too?"

"Heavens, no! I don't say it out loud around most people, but I figure if these turtles are as old as people say they are and they've been figuring out how to have babies all that time, they probably don't need my help." She shrugs at me and then stands. "However, I'm not one to miss a free circus, and this sure looks to be turning into one. Let's go!"

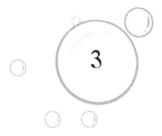

3

We skirt around the main beach area, with its big parking lots, restaurants, and skateboard park, in Annie's car. This end of the island is primarily older beach homes, a lot of them on stilts. A few look well maintained, but many have weedy, sandy yards; bleached-out paint; and tacked-on second-floor decks. The decks point to the ocean and probably get a glimpse of the waves over and between the other houses and dunes. On one of the sandy streets a block from the beach, we pull into a driveway.

"Whose house is this?"

"My Abigale's," Annie says. "You remember her, she's the lawyer that helped you and Craig out when his cousin got himself murdered. We'll park here for easier access to the beach."

Annie's getting out of the car, so I assume I should too. I pick my way through the thigh-high, flowering bushes and join her at the end of the driveway, where she looks upset. She starts stomping down the road before I can reach her, so I jog a couple steps to catch up.

"Are you okay?" I ask. "What's wrong?"

She lets out a frazzled puff of air. "It's convenient to park there, but it just makes me furious. That husband of hers imagines himself to be some surfer dude. She works so hard, and he can't even be bothered to take care of the house. All his accumulated toys mean she can't even pull up under the deck, and you'd think he could cut back some of the weeds." She blows out another loud breath and shakes her arms down at her side, which sets her bracelets jingling. "Abigale seems happy with him, but he just sets me off something fierce."

As we turn onto one of the streets heading toward the dunes, she points. "See? Right through there is where the fake nest is."

All along the street there are cars, and once we get closer we can see that there are even news vans. Voices rise over the rolling waves. As we climb the steps at the wooden beach walkover, we can see Annie was right. It is most definitely a circus.

Police and other official four-wheel vehicles are parked on the beach. Stakes with their ends painted bright red surround the mound of sand now and are encircled by several loops of neon-yellow caution tape. I'd left earlier before they took down the makeshift barrier. The woman Sheila has a group surrounding her, and she's still preaching, though it sounds as if her voice is beginning to give out. Thank goodness.

We can see Lucy surrounded by people in light-green shirts, which I recognize as the Turtle Tracker shirts. A gust of wind hits us, and Annie and I both turn away from the beach as our faces get blasted by the grit of sand. When the wind passes, we hurry down the walkway and onto the beach.

"Hopefully the wind won't be so bad down here," Annie says. We walk along the swaying sea oats and then skirt around the back of the marked nest to get to the side of the green-shirted folks. To be fair, there are also some folks wearing the green shirts on the opposite side with Sheila.

"Hi, girls," Lucy says as she dispenses her expected hugs. These hugs are tighter and a second longer than the ones I've come to expect. When she pulls back, she's wearing a tightlipped, serious expression. "Thank you for coming."

Annie shrugs at me and raises her eyebrows, but says nothing.

"Have they made any decision?" I ask.

Lucy sighs, and her shoulders fall. "To leave it as is. I suppose they're right. When nothing ever hatches, then we'll all know I was right. Until then we'll just have to survive being laughed at by whoever perpetrated this cruel hoax."

I pat Lucy's back, and then she looks up at me. "You probably think I'm being silly, but…"

Annie looks around at the fracas, the factions of green shirts that are forming. "Yeah, I kinda do."

Lucy scowls up at big, tall Annie. "You just don't get it. You never have. The turtles need us!"

Annie grabs her friend in a hug. "Oh no, sweetie. You know me, just trying to be funny. I'm sorry. I take this very seriously."

However, her rolling eyes at me over our friend's back do not match her words. "Lucy, honey," she says, "you should tell the TV newspeople exactly what you just told me. Go on the record."

Lucy pulls away and straightens the collar on her shirt. "I already did."

Annie's son Aiden walks up to us. He looks tired and hot and sandy. "Have you been here all morning?" I ask him.

He nods. "Yes, ma'am, but I think we're done here now. The site is secure, and the winds are picking up. There's supposed to be a storm this afternoon, so we'd like to get all these people off the beach." He sidles up to his mother. "Did y'all get down to talk to Eden?"

She nods and holds her hand up to him as if to tell him to be quiet, but he says to me, "Ms. Mantelle, Eden would be no trouble at all. Why, if Momma would let me, I'd move her right into the house with us."

Annie squawks. "Aiden Hopper Bryant, shut your mouth this minute!" She pulls him to the side and is giving him an earful when another gust of wind hits us. We all duck our heads for the sand to blow by, and shouts alert us that a striped umbrella is tumbling our way. It's bouncing off the sand, then up into the air, and instinctively everyone parts to avoid it. Instead of hitting any bystanders, the umbrella hits the line of caution tape strung around the nest. With another gust, it leaps the tape and skitters across the mound of sand, coming to land on the opposite side near us.

I bend down to grab it and latch onto the green stripe of the umbrella, which is closest to me. As Officer Bryant comes to take it out of my hand, I step to the side and look down where the umbrella's pointed end has come to rest. I squat down because I see something. Maybe a turtle was here after all. Maybe these are some of the eggs?

There's something beige in the sand, but it's also purple. My leaning forward to see better suddenly stops as I jerk back and fall on my bottom. I look up at Aiden where he's struggling to untangle the umbrella from the caution tape. "Officer, uh, Aiden—look!" He follows my pointing finger and my eyes; then he jerks back like I did.

There, on the edge of the mound, part of a foot with toenails painted a pretty lilac have been uncovered by the wind and the umbrella.

Well, I guess Lucy's right: we can safely assume this isn't a turtle nest.

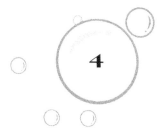

4

Electricity shoots through the crowd as word spreads. The news crews, who had been reporting from outside the circle to get a nice shot of the ocean in the background, aggressively shove through now, pushing and wiggling until Lucy, Annie, and I find ourselves behind them. Like everyone else, stunned horror claims our faces. Mouths hang open; eyebrows are flattened above wide open eyes. Someone throws up toward the dunes. That shakes up the police and emergency workers, and they begin pushing people away, widening the circle around the already caution-taped crime scene.

Lucy backs away and then grabs Annie's and my arms just as her legs weaken. Annie growls, "Let's go to the benches near the parking lot," and we head in that direction. Lucy is small, but it's still a struggle to get her across the sand. She starts whimpering, and by the time we get to the nearest ocean-facing bench, she's crying.

Annie hugs her and I pat her back as we sit and watch the crowd ebb and flow. Emergency vehicles with lights flashing roar up the beach from both directions. Loud voices shout instructions, but the actual words are lost to us on the rising wind.

I spit grit, then speak from behind my hand. "We can't talk out here. Sand keeps getting in my mouth from just breathing."

With a deep sigh, Lucy pushes on our knees to stand. "Let's go inside The Dunes before the storm hits."

We hurry along the sidewalk into the restaurant named The Dunes, which is right on the edge of the beach. A recent renovation makes it look like it's tucked underneath a pier when it's actually a free-standing building with a wide deck situated on the sandy beach. Even so, concrete beams protrude from the ceiling, looking like they hold up an old pier with markings for wave height and places for boats to dock, but which are all fake. From inside, thanks to large windows and glass doors, and from the outside deck, diners have a view all the way down to the waves. We aren't the only ones brushing ourselves off and stomping our shoes to rid ourselves of sand before entering the double doors. Although, being on the beach, the restaurant staff are probably used to a little sand. Lucy staggers over to a small table in the corner of the large room. She's already seated by the time Annie and I get there.

"I can't get it out of my head. I stood over a body all morning—fighting! Arguing. Shouting." Lucy shudders and then says to a waitress only just heading in our direction, "I need a glass of wine."

"Water for me," I say, and Annie nods her agreement. The waitress nods and swings toward another table that's just been seated. A quick glance at those patrons tells me they're just as shaken as we are.

"There they are!"

I look up to see Tamela and our other friend Cherry rushing across the room. They pull up chairs at our table and look at us, especially at Lucy, with their eyes stretched wide.

Tamela wraps one arm around Lucy before she sits down. "I'm so sorry I wasn't there, hon. I just had to go home and get something to eat. I could feel my blood sugar dropping, and then I went by to pick up Cherry. I do feel bad about waking you up," she says to Cherry as she sits on the edge of her wooden chair.

Cherry shakes her head. "No, I'm glad you did. I usually only crash for a few hours after my shift, so it was almost time to get up." Cherry is a nurse. She works on weekend evenings at the local hospital. Since last night was Sunday, she was in bed when all the excitement happened this morning. "So tell us what happened," she says. "We walked up and couldn't believe all the police cars with their lights flashing. We still thought it was just about the turtle nest."

Annie crosses her arms and huffs. "Someone did that intentionally. Buried that poor girl there and then marked it like a nest!"

Lucy starts and looks at Annie. "Girl? It's a girl? I couldn't look, but you saw enough to know that?"

Annie and I meet eyes, then nod at Lucy. I explain quietly, "The toenails were painted light purple."

Tamela moans, and Lucy's eyes fill with tears. She jumps up and runs to the bathroom. Cherry follows her, saying over her shoulder, "its okay. I've got her."

The waitress steps up from the other side of the restaurant to deliver our drinks. "Brought water for your friends," she says. "Does anyone want anything else?"

Annie looks up at her. "Yes. An order of fries to share." As the waitress leaves, Annie says, "I need some starch, and it looks like the storm is getting ready to hit. We might be here a while."

Tamela leans toward us. "The police were moving fast when we came by the site. They'd thrown up a canopy and they had the body uncovered. We couldn't see much, but it was a girl or young woman. Just so sad."

"I can't get over someone being so cold as to bury her and then put up all that garbage to mark her grave." Annie waves her hand and looks around. "I need a straw. Can't believe they make you ask for one now." She catches a waiter's attention and yells out her request. All around the room, others echo her desire, and the young man scurries around handing out straws. "Ice water makes my teeth hurt," Annie explains to him. "You're a sweetheart!"

"But all that garbage and the mound of sand kept anyone from looking for evidence of a crime," I say. A loud clap of thunder precedes a deluge of rain, and we all look out the window nearest us. "If there was any evidence left, it won't last long in this."

"Hope Aiden and the other officers don't get in any trouble." Annie bites her lips, then whispers, "I mean, they spent hours walking around a murder scene." She frowns. "It has to be a murder, right? Her buried like that?"

Tamela and I nod as Lucy and Cherry return to the table.

Lucy takes a sip of her wine, then takes a deep breath. "I heard the word 'murder.' Of course it's a murder. Has anyone heard of any missing persons this morning?"

Cherry shakes her head. "Nothing when I left the hospital, but that was really early."

"What happened to the cooler and beer bottles that were marking the nest?" I ask. "Maybe there were fingerprints."

Lucy and Tamela inhale sharply. Tamela chokes out, "Mine! I helped move that stuff."

"Mine too," Lucy says. "We put it in garbage bags that someone had from walking on the beach this morning. You know how we pick up trash as we walk. I suppose someone carried them home to throw away or found a trash can. Oh my, the police sure have their work cut out for them."

Cherry lays down her phone with a sigh. "Y'all know my youngest daughter,

Jo, moved back home after her Christmas break? Taking a break from school." As the comment's accented by rolling eyes, I'm not sure her mother thinks Jo's going back to school any time soon. "Anyway, apparently there was a huge group of college kids camping out and partying down at Peele's Point this weekend. Most of them are from South Georgia College, where she went. That's why she was there." Cherry taps the back of her phone with her finger. "Jo says there were some fights, and on Facebook people are looking for a couple that didn't show up back at school. She heard about the body on the beach, and she's wondering if she should call the police."

We all nod, and Annie speaks up. "Absolutely she should. Maybe this will wrap up quickly if she does."

Cherry shrugs. "But she says she doesn't know them. She's just seen things on Facebook."

"Let me text Aiden," Annie says. "Tell him we have something for him."

My eyes fly to Lucy. We learned with the last investigation that Aiden often ignores his mother's texts.

Lucy winks at me. "Honey, you know

he'll just think you're texting him to see if he's out in the rain. Why don't I text him?"

Annie sniffs. "That probably true. I know he ignores my texts. If he only understood that's why I have to barge on in all the time! Oh, here's our fries."

The large platter of fries smells heavenly. We all take one, but end up putting them back on the edge of the plate because they're so hot. All around us, tables are getting food. The rain seems to be slacking off, but we're supposed to have rain all day. The fries seem to lift our spirits. Halfway through the platter, we've stopped talking about murder and intrigue and have moved on to the upcoming shrimp festival when a man approaches our table, clearing his throat.

Lucy, Annie, and Cherry all wrinkle their noses and exchange quick looks, and then Lucy straightens herself and cocks her head at him. "Detective Johnson. What can we do for you?"

The detective has on a full trench coat, and I realize I haven't seen one of those since I moved to Florida. Up north I saw them all the time. His is covered in rain droplets, and his thin, dark hair is plastered to his head, wet and shiny. He stares around the table like a teacher taking roll. When he gets to Tamela he stops. "Your name, madam?"

Her voice quavers as she breathes, "Tamela Stout."

He stares at her as if imprinting her into his brain. Abruptly his eyes shift to me. "You're that Mantelle woman who got messed up in that murder of her cousin earlier this year, correct?"

"He wasn't *my* cousin," I explain.

He smirks and looks back at Lucy. "What is this you texted young Bryant about knowing the victim?"

Lucy smirks back at him. She holds out a hand at Annie, who is ready to come out of her seat and fight the man. There was no disguising the disgust in his voice when he said, "Young Bryant."

Lucy uses her boss voice, saying, "I informed Officer Bryant of a possible connection to a group of students from South Georgia College who were here over the weekend. All we know is what is on Facebook, so maybe you should skedaddle back to your office and do some actual detective work."

I look back up at him expecting him to be red-faced and mad. He looks like the type to have a short fuse. Instead he's smiling at Lucy, and he reaches out a hand to squeeze her shoulder. "Of course, Lucy. You ladies can rest assured I'll have this matter wrapped up in no time."

Lucy shrugs her shoulder to dislodge his hand, but he leaves it in place.

Then, with another quick squeeze and a wink, he turns and leaves.

"That man!" she says with a shudder. She downs the remainder of her wine.

Annie laughs. "He knows you've still got it for him bad!"

"Shut your mouth! It was one stupid date before I really knew him."

Cherry's eyes pop open wide, and I can feel mine do the same. "You went out with him?" I ask.

"Once," Lucy sniffs, "as a favor to the mayor. When we were hiring him, he was in town for the interview and he's attractive from a distance. Believe me, it didn't take long for me to figure him out. He's just plain old creepy."

Annie leans on the table, her eyes shining. "And he's been pining for you ever since. It must be true love."

"More like lust," Tamela spits out of the side of her mouth. "I think he's scary."

Lucy shakes her head. "He's manageable. Actually comes in handy at times."

"What?" I ask incredulously.

"Oh, for parking passes and such. And if we're going to be investigating this crime…"

Annie sighs. "That's true. Last time he was out of town so we could get information from Aiden and Charlie. You know, Officer Greyson."

"Oh! Oh, he's the man Officer Greyson warned me about," I say, a fry loaded with ketchup halfway to my mouth. "He said something like he was a good cop but not a good detective?"

"That's the one," Annie says. "He wants things wrapped up fast. He doesn't like actually having to think." She stretches to look out the window, where sunshine is lighting up the humidity-fogged windows. "Looks like a break in the weather, but honestly I don't know what we could possibly investigate this time, Lucy. Sounds like it's a lovers' quarrel, and once they find her boyfriend, it'll wrap up. Sad, but probably not that uncommon."

"Could be," Lucy says as we all gather our things and finish our drinks. "One thing concerns me, though. Would a boy who wasn't from the beach think of hiding the body in a turtle nest? Especially when there aren't any around? Also, isn't a lovers' quarrel passionate? Seems a little too cool for a college-age boyfriend to think of hiding her body like that."

We all think for a minute, and then Annie sighs and stands. "Or you're just wanting to work a case with your old beau, Detective Johnson." She laughs, then ducks out of the way to avoid getting slapped.

"I'd say it again, but I know it's just not possible," Lucy says as she prances away from our table.

Annie looks in her direction. "What's not possible?"

Lucy swirls around and, with a sweet smile, announces loudly, "You shutting your mouth!"

This time there's a whole restaurant to laugh with us. Annie pouts for a moment, then joins the laughter.

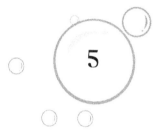

5

When I left the house this morning, walking to Sophia Coffee, my plan had been to not come home quite this early. I'd thought Annie could drop me off at the library, where I'd spend a couple of hours looking for more mystery books now that I'm hooked on them. The cozy mystery series are set in neat places with interesting but regular people as characters. My new friends here introduced me to them. Their love for the genre is what made them want to investigate crimes, like they did when Craig's cousin was murdered.

The two series I've been reading are set at opposite ends of the country. The Death on Demand series by Carolyn Hart is set on the South Carolina coast while the series by

Diane Mott Davidson featuring Goldy Bear Catering is set high in the mountains of Colorado. I wanted to try some by M.C. Beaton, who has two mystery series set overseas that my friends all love. I thought I'd find a comfy chair and read there for a while.

However, Annie also wanted to stop into the library, but real quick, so I grabbed *The Quiche of Death*, the first by Ms. Beaton in her Agatha Raisin series, and caught a ride home with Annie. It's not currently raining, so my full-size umbrella serves as a walking stick as I enter the open gates guarding our property. They are big, black iron gates that stayed locked before our arrival, even before Craig's aunt Corabelle checked herself into a sanitarium a couple of decades ago. Craig spent summers here with her as a kid and teenager, but after that she pushed him away any time he reached out to her, and then, well, he just forgot about her. I'm afraid that might be a part of Craig's personality I wasn't completely aware of, but I'm becoming more familiar with his "outta sight, outta mind" mentality every day.

When Aunt Cora left him this house we jumped—okay, I jumped—at the chance to start over in a new place. Craig was retiring, and my nest was finally empty. We moved around a lot as Craig moved up the engineering consulting ladder, so I haven't worked outside the home in years. My life focused completely on our four kids, so another move felt at least a bit familiar whereas the empty nest did not. Plus, Craig and I were steadily moving apart. A change could only help, right?

It wasn't until we were in the middle of the murder investigation that I found out that we're stuck here in this house for five years. However, as Annie pointed out earlier, Craig doesn't exactly seem to be stuck here. Just me.

Living here sure hasn't helped heal our marriage. It feels like I'm the only one with any hope for us. Craig really hates Sophia Island and this house. If I'm honest, though, he was done with our marriage before we even set foot in Florida. Even in counseling he didn't seem to have a good reason.

So, I just don't think about it.

I jump at a loud boom of thunder, and it spurs me to hurry up the path to the front steps. It's all I can do to not cry thinking about spending a stormy afternoon alone here. However there are some bright spots. The front porch is covered in what I found out is jasmine. The vines covering the porch and most of the side bushes have been absolutely loaded with fragrant, white flowers. They look to be dying out, but the smell is intoxicating, if not somewhat overpowering, so Southern and springlike. Our lot is huge with many old trees with low limbs and tons of Spanish moss. The house is also huge, with three floors of grimy windows, faded paint, rotting boards, and sad, dirty chimney bricks. Honestly, I can't blame Craig for taking one look at this place and begging his old employer to put him on that long-term project in South Florida.

There's another boom of thunder. I hear the wind picking up again and then the sound of rain headed in my direction. I rush up the front steps, unlock the front door, and wrestle it open. A waft of jasmine comes in with me, along with the smell of rain, but those delightful smells don't mask the old smell of the house. They just add a layer over it like perfume on person who doesn't like to bathe.

I bang my umbrella point in frustration on the floor next to me. This is just not fair, Craig saddling me with all this.

My phone rings, and I dig it out of my purse. It's my daughter, Erin, and I rush to answer. "Hey there. How are you feeling?"

Erin is five months pregnant. She and her husband, Paul, live in St. Louis, and this is their first baby.

"I'm good. I just get so tired, so I try and rest at lunch time. I don't know how people do it working in an office when they're pregnant."

"It is nice that you work from home."

"Where are you? It's noisy there."

"I'm home. We're having a huge storm. I never realized how often it storms at the beach. They all take it for granted, and then what's even crazier is there's never puddles or mud. Water just drains through the sand, I guess."

"Well, I can't wait to see this paradise. We bought tickets for Memorial Day!"

She practically yells this, and I know I'm supposed to act surprised. And happy. I finally choke out, "Really?"

"Yeah, with the baby not due until early August I'll be fine to fly. Sadie and Jared are planning on driving so they can stop and see his sister in Atlanta. They figure driving will be easier with Carver. He'll be, what, like a year and half? That would be a nightmare on a plane, I guess."

"Sadie and Jared are coming too?"

Erin waits, then speaks carefully. "That

was always the plan, right? The boys will be done with school, and we're all coming to see you and Dad and the *family mansion*." After a bit of a laugh, she pauses before asking, "Is everything okay?"

I look around at all the old furniture packed into this place, the dark curtains and filthy windows. The old, dusty carpets are barely fit to walk on, much less let Carver play on. Distracted I mumble, "Have you told your dad?"

"Seriously, Mom. He's on a job. You know he barely makes sense on the phone anyway and definitely not in the middle of a project. What's going on? You sound really strange."

I've never been a talker. I'm really good at keeping my feelings inside. I was raised to never complain and to never share family business with anyone—even other family members. However, that is not how my friends here operate, and, well…

"You got a minute?" I ask my daughter, and then I sit down on the settee.

This could take some time.

By the time my call with Erin is over, the storm has ended too. Seaside storms seem to be particularly fierce, but then they vanish out to sea, leaving nary a trace behind. Sunlight sparkles on the grass and leaves and jasmine blossoms, but there is no sparkle from the pile of fabric piled next to me on the front porch, fabric that tended to disintegrate when I yanked it down from the windows. I'm sure these curtains cost a pretty penny when Corabelle bought them, or even when possibly her parents bought them, but they are completely worthless now. My thrifty mindset began with me taking them down, cleaning them, and donating them somewhere, but then they started falling apart in my hands.

The sparkles of sunshine are joined by a sharp beep. I look up to see a truck backing into our yard. On the back of the truck is a dumpster, both sporting the logo of Plantation Services, a local cleaning company. Waving at me from the passenger seat, out her open window, is Annie. She sometimes dates the owner of Plantation Services, Ray Barnette, who is also a city councilman.

"Why, hello, Missus Mantelle," Ray calls from the driver's seat. "Pleased to see you made it through the afternoon storms unscathed." Ray Barnette is a Southern gentleman through and through. As stereotypical as it seems, on him it also feels sincere. Genuine. He's only a bit taller than me, though his full head of white hair might add a couple of inches. He's muscular for an older man, but he also has that paunch most men his age develop.

"Hey! Come get me down from here!" Annie shouts from where she's half hanging out the door of the big truck. She's wearing powder-blue capris, white tennis shoes, and a flowered top that is fitted at her shoulders and bust before flowing down past her hips. As I walk down the steps, Ray shuffles over to give her a hand and help her maneuver down. She's all smiles by the time I reach them. "I couldn't resist when Ray asked if I wanted to come along. Something about a man driving a big ol' truck." She winks and Ray blushes as he winks back at her.

"Plus I had to see with my own two eyes that you are actually starting to clean out this old place," she adds. "Lord help us, is that the curtains?"

We head toward the porch as I answer. "Yep, came apart in my hands. I only stopped sneezing a few minutes ago."

Ray walks to the rear of the truck. "So where do you want me to set this thing? Doesn't look as if we have to worry about killing any grass."

"No," I say with a sigh. "It's pretty patchy. Mostly just sand. Wherever you think is best."

He continues to look around, then heads back to the driver's seat while Annie follows me back up the front steps. She says, "Eden called. She said you're ready for her to move in immediately? So Craig approved?"

I shrug and then shove open the door. "I don't know. We'll see, if he ever calls me back. I left a message for him that we need to talk. Usually I chase him down until I catch him, but this time if he wants to know what's going on, he'll have to call me."

She laughs but only pats me on my back as we walk farther into the house. We look around, and then she sneezes.

"This place is still full of dust, I guess. Sorry."

"But it feels lighter already," Annie says. "The windows are still dirty and the bushes overgrown, but well, it's a start. What happened? Why today?"

I roll my eyes at her. "My kids are coming for Memorial Day. All of them. We hadn't told them anything, and you know young people. They're busy with their own lives, and well, we kind of, well, lied about how life is here." I force my voice to pick up volume and cheer. "It's all good, it's paradise, it's fun!" I reach over and pull at a strip of falling wallpaper. "I sent them pictures of the river or the beach, talked about my new friends. Craig, I guess, just talked about his project. Everything was very superficial. Until today." The wallpaper breaks off in my hand, and I throw it onto the chair sitting beside me, which is slowly filling up with pieces of wallpaper. Finally talking with Erin felt good. Although I hate how I laid all my worries on her at one time, it was high time I opened up. Past time. I couldn't let her get here next month thinking her daddy and I were great.

Annie looks around, her hands on her hips. "It's good you finally did something. You've spent too much time wondering where to start. Eden has a lot of energy, so she'll be good for you." We hear metal scraping against metal in the yard and turn toward the door. "And remember," Annie says with a smile, "with Eden comes Aiden on his days off. He's a good worker, too, if you have a list ready."

"Have you heard anything else from him about that girl at the beach?" I ask.

In the yard, Ray is pulling the truck up, away from my temporary dumpster.

"Aiden says Johnson has passed it off to

the authorities at the college. He's already taken everything down at the site and closed the book on it."

"So it was that poor girl. How awful for her family. I can't imagine."

Annie shakes her head, and we both sigh. "Me either. I just wonder where her boyfriend is. I'm sure they'll find him soon."

"Your chariot awaits, Miss Annie," Ray yells as we come out onto the porch.

"Wait," I say, jogging down the steps. "Don't I need to sign a contract or pay a deposit?"

He waves a hand at me. "Naw, just holler when you're through with it, and I'll write you up a bill. Not like you're going to take off with it, right?" He laughs and gives Annie a boost up into the truck. He pats her ample, powder-blue behind, and she squeals.

He runs around the cab to his door, laughing and telling her to save him a seat. Young love is overrated. These two, this older couple, they make me smile. The Spanish moss hanging from the big tree at the gate makes me smile. That jasmine, with its perfect, creamy white flowers, makes me smile. My hand on the banister that's been touched by people for decades, the idea of little Carver walking up steps his ancestors built, makes me smile.

Over and over since we've been here I've told myself it'll all be okay. That I'll be okay.

However, this is the first time I've actually believed myself.

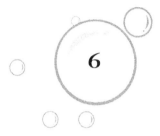

6

"You don't have to be a part of the Turtle Trackers, but you have to be a part of something!" Tamela preaches to me and Cherry. I let Cherry have the front seat. She's no more than an inch taller than me, but her legs are a mile long. I'm in the back seat of Tamela's little car, and we are bouncing over the railroad tracks headed to the opposite end of the marina from my house.

This end is more industrial. The port is at the very end, and before it lie some old warehouses. Some are falling down, but those have the best waterfront view. There was talk recently about them being torn down and a big condo with marina access being built. They call them "dockominiums." For that to happen, though, the city would have to sell the marina to a private company. Craig was actually in talks to be the dockominium manager, but the plan fell apart when it came to light that his cousin, who had married into the private management company, died before he could sell them. What a disaster that would've been for not only the town, but my budding social life, since my friends were all opposed. However, since it came with a dockominium to live in, I guess we would've had a pretty cool view to be miserable in front of.

There are cars lining all the streets, and as Tamela cruises, looking for a spot, she gives us a rundown of the groups that put together tonight's emergency meeting. "There's the Turtle Trackers and the Tree Conservancy; Marina Forever; and Keep It Simple, Sophia, which we all call KISS. Then there's the merchant group, which is kind of new. They don't have a cool name yet. There's another couple of beach groups: one for the beaches in the city and the other for the beaches in the county. There's the people that live up on the bluff, where the first settlement by the Spanish was. We just call it The Settlement. Their group is officially called The Historic Settlement Preservation Association."

Cherry leans to the side and looks back

at me during Tamela's lecture. She gives me a smirk and then turns back to our driver to ask her, "How long have you lived here?"

Tamela is pulling into a spot near the library. Her tongue is pressing on her bottom lip in concentration. "Oh, almost twenty years. Hert moved here with the paper mill, and we knew it would be a perfect place to retire. There are lots of us retired paper mill folks here. Just like all the military people that get stationed in this area and then stay." She turns the car off and opens the door.

Over the top of the car she points at us as we close our doors. "You have to stay on top of things here or we'll turn into just another Daytona or Orlando!"

Cherry gives me another smile. "Okay. We'll see."

Tamela sees a lady across the street from us. She's headed in the same direction with her light-green turtle shirt on, so Tamela motions that she's going to walk with her. Cherry grabs my forearm to keep me on our side of the street. "Don't look so scared," she says to me under her breath.

"Do I?" I shake my head. "I can't help it. I'm not used to all this. Tamela shamed me into coming. I finally got going on the house,

Eden is moving in tonight, and here I am. Where I definitely do not want to be."

"Don't worry. I won't let you join anything tonight. I wouldn't be here except I throw Tamela and Lucy a bone every so often to keep them happy. They love belonging to these groups, and the groups all have great missions and lots of passion, but they're not for everyone." I follow her as we keep walking back toward the marina. "I know it's good to volunteer. I'd just rather do it one on one with people, like at the free medical clinic. You might like tutoring at-risk kids. But there's no hurry to decide." She rolls her eyes and pats my hand. "You just got here!"

Tamela hadn't really given me a choice when she told me she'd be picking me up for tonight's meeting. She'd rushed in her explanation, but it was spurred by how things were handled with the fake turtle nest this morning. As far as I understand it, the Turtle Trackers felt they needed to make a statement and come up with a plan for handling fake nests. The county beach group was upset about the college kids making a mess on the beach over the weekend, much less causing a murder. The city beach group felt the trash cans on the beach contributed the garbage that was used to mark the fake nest and wanted to reevaluate them. Anyway, they all felt an emergency meeting was necessary.

Tamela and Lucy felt Cherry and I being there was necessary. They said Annie was a lost cause.

As we come to the last street to cross, Cherry points up to the second floor of the restaurant in front of us. "The meeting is up there. Second floor of The Crab Pot. It's one of the oldest buildings in town."

As we enter, it's obvious there will be way more people upstairs than on the main floor, where only a couple of tables are taken. I've not eaten here yet, but it looks familiar, like a seafood place from my childhood. Smells like one too. Climbing the staircase goes slowly with the crowd, and when we come out at the top, it's to a room full of people. Most are gathered in groups according to their color-coordinated T-shirts. We head toward the green shirts, Tamela and her friend leading the way. As far as I can see among the standing-room-only crowd, the floor is all glossy wood, with old wood walls that have been layered with varnish many times over the years. Fishing nets stretch along walls, artfully arranged around dozens of pictures. Some are of groups of people. Many are framed newspaper articles, and then there are the requisite maps. They are all accented with a layer of dust.

I follow Tamela closely until I'm physically turned to my right and through a doorway by Cherry. She whispers in my ear, "The bar."

Tucked against the wall is indeed a bar. Every stool is taken, but Cherry heads down to the opening at the end and holds up a twenty-dollar bill. In the same voice I bet she would announce a code blue at the hospital she says, "Three chardonnays." The bartender nods at her, and in just a matter of moments we are back on our original path, now with three glasses of wine.

"I got one for Tamela since she did drive us. If she doesn't want it, we'll split it." She winks at me, and I laugh. So far my first emergency meeting isn't off to a bad start.

Cherry and I lean against the side wall underneath a huge, mounted swordfish. It also has the requisite layer of dust, but, as Cherry pointed out, we're not in danger of the dust falling on us as it's captured by years of grease particles from all the fried seafood cooked in the kitchen.

Lucy only has time to nod a quick hello to us as she's busy talking strategy with other green-shirted people and sometimes with the leaders of the other groups. To our right, front, and center are the city commissioners—or are they councilmembers? Or is that the same thing? They haven't said anything to the assembly, but have talked to each other and to the people that come to them. Even they are dressed in what I guess is called "island casual", though there is one young man wearing a pretty nice suit and tie. However, since there are no empty seats behind the table I don't think he's actually on the council.

He's leaning on the table and speaking rather loudly. All I can make out, though, is something about "Ruining our beach!"

The councilmembers are focused on him, but then Councilwoman Sheryl-Lee King gives him a withering look as she says even louder, "Exactly how long have you even lived here? *Our* beach?" The rest of the councilmembers laugh and leave the young man out to dry as they turn to talk to each other. Sheryl-Lee preens in in her tight Shrimp Fest T-shirt. She's much younger than the other councilmembers and is not really a nice person at all. She's good friends with one of Annie's daughter, the one that's not that nice of a person either.

At that center table, along with Sheryl-Lee, there's Ray Barnette, my dumpster deliveryman. As I sip on chardonnay, I think that it's kind of cool that I know two councilmembers already, but then I remember that I only know them because my husband was a murder suspect.

Craig. I move to pull my phone out of my pocket, wondering if he might've returned my call. Nope, but I do have several texts. I groan, and Cherry asks what's wrong.

"Oh, I filled my daughter Erin in on how things are here with me and her dad and the house. Apparently, she spread the word to my other children."

My older son, Chris, sent an emoji of a scrunched-up face and arms raised in confusion. Then he added a couple of question marks in case I didn't get the message.

Our younger boy, Drew, sent a long, rambling text with every other word misspelled, and I don't feel like deciphering it right now. Erin's twin, Sadie, Carver's mom, made an appointment to talk tomorrow at ten thirty-five a.m. Sadie believes in appointments. I click through to do some more scrolling as the meeting moves on without me.

Tamela suddenly jumps up from her seat. I watch as she maneuvers through the crowd to get to Lucy. She shows her something on her phone at just about the same time I see others reaching for their phones. There are several gasps, and I look at Cherry, who pulls her phone from her back pocket and looks at it. "Text from my daughter. Oh no…"

"What?"

She taps away at her phone as she shakes her head. "The couple that was missing? They're not missing. They were holed up in some motel outside Savannah. He didn't kill her," she says as she holds up a Facebook post of a boy carrying a girl in his arms. "He married her."

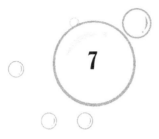

7

"By the time we get back to your car, I'll practically be home," I say to Tamela as we slowly make our way down The Crab Pot's stairs. The meeting broke up pretty quickly, with everyone staring at their phones and reading the community's Facebook pages. Cherry pointed those Facebook pages out to me, so I joined them all, even the kind of crazy ones. She says those are the most fun to lurk in.

"As long as you never, ever post anything on there or even comment," Tamela says over her shoulder. "That's like throwing a big ol' ham shank into a pool of piranhas. They will strip you clean in the blink of an eye. And as for you walking home, there's a murderer out there!"

"It's not even dark. I'll be careful. Besides, it'll take forever to drive back to that side of Centre Street with all these people." Outside, little groups form and people stand around, even in the crosswalk, talking. Everyone is wondering who the dead girl is and how the police made such a huge mistake.

Lucy finds us just as I'm convincing Tamela I'll be fine walking home. "There you are!" she says. "Can you believe this disaster? Detective Johnson was in such a hurry to wrap everything up. He has to be fired! The commissioners are fit to be tied!"

Cherry nods. "They sure were in a hurry to get out of here. Speaking of which," she turns to Tamela and adds, "ready to go?"

Cherry doesn't live downtown, so she needs a ride home. I don't, so I say goodbye, ignore Tamela's worries, and stride down the sidewalk.

It's a pretty night, so even though it's Monday, there are lots of people out and about. This is the first time I've ever lived in a historic or touristy town. Everything is so charming and inviting: softly lit restaurants with outside seating; music, usually from a live band, swirls around. Even the smell from the paper mill adds a bit of seasoning. Tamela has explained they only make brown paper and cardboard here. The horrible smells associated with paper mills, she says, is from the production of white paper, something about the extra chemicals necessary to bleach the paper.

The squawks of seagulls and the expanse of orange sky pull me to look toward the marina as I cross Centre Street. I can see the river topped with the last strip of colorful sky, as the sun set a while ago. I turn up the sidewalk to walk down the street with the ice cream store on the corner, and it brings a big smile to my face.

Wait till Carver finds out there's an ice cream shop within walking distance of Gigi and Papa's house. I look back down the busy street before I turn the corner, and my smile grows. The kids are going to love this. They are going to love Sophia Island.

Entering the darker area away from the businesses, a breeze chills me for a moment. That poor girl, dying on the beach. It just doesn't seem right for such a happy place. I pick up my pace and am quickly turning up our drive where it's wonderful to see the lights are on.

"Eden?" I say as I enter the front door.

"Hey!" She pops out of the kitchen. "You said to make myself at home, so I am. Can I get you a beer? I brought some groceries, and I was just going out to sit on the porch with that delicious-smelling jasmine."

"Sure. I'll take a beer." She hands me the bottle in her hand and goes back to get another from the fridge. She also grabs a bag of pita chips, and we head to the porch with its odd assortment of inside furniture.

Eden's slouchy gym pants hang low on her hips. She has on an old, worn sweater. It's a dark pink and is cut off to show her midriff. I sit in one of the wooden chairs, and she plops down onto a low, cushioned chair. She crosses her feet up into the chair with her, then opens the bag of chips. I go to twist off the cap of my bottle, but see it's not a twist-off.

"Oh, here." She pulls a bottle opener out of her pants pocket. "I saw you have some of that light-beer stuff with twist-off caps, but yeah, I don't do that." She wrinkles up her nose as she opens my beer and hands it back to me. "You'll love this. It's local."

I also wrinkle my nose because I know I will probably not like this beer. My kids are beer snobs, too, but since she's already got the cap off, I'll try.

"Aiden was here," she says. "Can you believe it wasn't that college girl? Now I'm worried again that it'll be someone I know. You didn't see her face, did you?"

"No." I take a tiny sip of the beer and try to not grimace at the bitter taste. "How does Aiden think the mix-up happened?"

"Just people in a hurry and the missing couple fit perfectly with what everyone wanted: to not know the victim. Listen"—she continues talking as she munches on the chips—"I started looking at the furniture. Most of it is a bust, but I'm going to put stickers on the bottom that let you know if it's something you should keep or donate. Okay?"

Eden loves antiques, especially furniture, and had offered the first time I met her to help me do some sorting. Honestly, I'm still a little shocked I let her move in. Craig doesn't even know yet. Eden's speedily talking about the furniture, and I'm speedily beginning to hyperventilate. This is not at all like me to make all these decisions. With just a glance up I can see the dumpster on the side of the house. Oh my. What is Craig going to think about that? Who knew it would be so big? Who in the world is going to fill it? And with what? I can't just start throwing his aunt

Corabelle's things away! What was I thinking?

"Miss Jewel? Hey." Eden is leaning forward, waving at me.

"Oh, I'm sorry. Guess my mind wandered."

She sets the bag of chips on the table beside her. "No worries. Just going to get another beer. Looks like you're ready too. Told you it was good, didn't I?" She reaches out her hand.

"I still have…" But as I lift up my bottle, I realize it's empty. "Oh, I guess I liked it more than I thought I would, but no, thanks. I'm good." She walks back into the living room, our bottles in hand, and I lean back, my head resting against the front wall of the house.

The remaining light of dusk finds the cascades of white flowers surrounding me. They stand out against the darkening air. The wine from earlier and the fast-drunk beer have pushed all my questions away. I search for that anxious feeling, and it's gone. Evaporated. Taking a deep sniff of the night air, heavy with jasmine and sand, I startle when my phone rings. I pull it from my pocket, and all those questions leap to the front of my mind as I read the name on the screen.

I tap the red button and put the phone in my pocket.

Craig is not going to ruin this moment.

I tip my head toward the open door and shout, "Eden, I think I will have another beer."

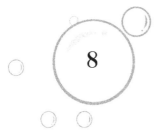

8

"You do not need any more furniture, Mom," Aiden says as his mother turns over another small table in my front room. She holds it up in the morning light to see the sticker. Eden told her about her system when she got here.

Annie gives him an evil side-eye. "If you ever move out, I'll have plenty of room."

He turns red and then goes back to rolling up the rug from the living room floor.

Eden and I look at each other and shrug as we share a smile. Annie showed up early this morning, having heard that her son was coming here before his shift. She brought pastries and fruit from Publix, so no one complained too much. Just a tip: I believe Publix grocery stores should have their own chapter in Florida handbooks. For one thing, if you bought it at Publix, you *say* you bought it at Publix, not just the grocery store. It's like the Good Housekeeping Seal of Approval or the polo guy on a Lacoste shirt.

With the rug rolled up, we all walk over the old wooden floor, examining it. It's dull, but it looks to be in good shape. Aiden's phone rings loudly, and I cringe as I say, "I have noticed without the curtains and now without the carpet, noise really carries in here."

He answers his phone after he steps out onto the front porch. Annie whispers at me and Eden, "Has he said anything about the girl on the beach?"

We both shake our heads as Eden picks up her little purse and slides it over her head so it hangs crossways over her chest. "I have to get to work. I already told them I'd be late, but the big tippers come in around nine, so I don't want to miss that." We watch as she stops on the porch and kisses Aiden on the cheek while he's still on the phone.

"Jewel, I so appreciate you letting her move in here," Annie says. "I'm trying to light a fire under that boy's behind for him to ask her to marry him. If she signs some kind of lease she can't get out of, it might slow things down." She folds her arms and looks around her. "She's a worker for sure. This place is a mess."

"It sure is. I can actually see all the dirt now."

"Jane Doe. Is there anything sadder that that?" Annie says with a sigh. "I can't get that purple polish out of my head. Makes her real, you know?"

"I know." It's all I was able to think about before falling asleep last night.

"Okay, I'm going to go," Aiden says as he steps back inside. "I'll run by the house and walk Oscar."

His mom asks, "Anything else on the girl?"

He shakes his head, then shrugs. "Not really. She does have a couple tattoos, so I'm going to be taking pictures of those around." He grimaces and adds, "One is a sea turtle, so I bet she's from the coast."

"Oh," I groan. "That's awful. Knowing that—and for her to be buried in a fake turtle nest."

We pause for a moment, and then Aiden steps up to Annie and kisses her cheek. "See you later, Mom. Bye, Miss Jewel."

He's out the door and down the sidewalk when she yells, "Don't forget Oscar!"

His "I won't" echoes back to us.

"I didn't know you had a dog." I pick up my coffee cup to refill it.

"*I* don't. It's Amber's." Annie puts a bit of sweetener in her coffee cup and waits for mine to fill. "Amber's putting in new hardwood floors in the rental house she and the kids moved into when she left Mark, so she asked us to keep Oscar for a few days. He's huge and hairy, but Annabelle, my youngest who also still lives at home, loves him. Wouldn't surprise me if we end up keeping him." Now that my coffee is done, she pushes the buttons to fill her own cup.

"Amber has kids, right? Wouldn't they miss him?"

Annie rolls her big, blue eyes at me. "Since she and her husband separated, the kids are at my house as much as theirs." Before taking a sip, she asks, "Have you met Amber?"

"Nope. We just parked a few times at her real estate office."

"Next time remind me, and we'll go in and see her. Although she's rarely there. So, what's on your agenda for today?"

"I'm going to start washing the insides of the windows," I say. "Has to be done some time, right? But first I'm going to sweep the living room and hallway now that the carpet is up."

We sit down at the kitchen table, which is crowded with knickknacks Eden removed from the living room, to enjoy our coffee. I ask, "How about you? What are you doing today?"

"Volunteering at the kids' school for the book fair, then picking up the grandkids from school so they can work on their science fair exhibits." She exhales and rolls her eyes again. "Which of course has to be done at my house since Amber is getting new floors."

"How old are they?" I ask.

"Leah is seven and Markie is six, both smart as whips."

"Does their dad live around here?"

Annie gives me a sour look. "Yes. He's from out in the country. *Way* out in the country." She takes a long drink of her coffee. "I have to admit, he always told Amber he wouldn't leave that farm. She's such a steam roller she just knew she'd move him right over here to the island." She stands and takes her cup to the sink. "Mark is exactly what he is, and I think instead of accepting that, Amber saw it as a challenge."

I turn in my chair toward her. "It's strange when our kids grow up and make their own families, isn't it? We only have the one grandson, but there's another one on the way in August." I join her at the sink. "Can't wait to have Carver here to visit next month."

Annie nods and then goes to the front door with me following. Over her shoulder she says, "Keep those pastries and fruit. I have a feeling Aiden will be eating over here a lot. And good luck with your cleaning. All this actually makes going to an elementary school look like fun!" She ends with a blast of laughter as she lumbers out the front door.

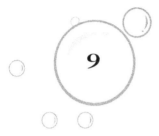

9

"I thought you were working the book fair?" I say when I open the door to find Annie standing on my porch midmorning. She's wringing her hands and taking quick looks over her shoulder at her car. She pushes me back and comes with me to stand just inside the door.

"The kids are in the car, so I can't come inside. Aiden just called me. The girl. The body? It's Leslie Callahan." She moans and leans against the doorjamb.

The name means nothing to me. "Do I know her?"

Annie lowers her head, then looks back up at me with her head cocked on an angle. "No." She shakes her head and sighs. "That's probably why I came here. She's kind of family. Amber's mostly ex-sister-in-law, and, well, she was always kind of wild. Folks don't think kindly of the Callahans, and I knew you wouldn't think one way or the other."

"Grandma, Markie's eating his lunch," a little girl announces from the bottom of the porch steps.

Annie startles, then spins to face her granddaughter. "Lord help us! Leah, you about scared me to death. Get back in that car."

Instead the little girl begins climbing the stairs. As she looks around with big eyes, she asks, "Is this house haunted?" Like a flash, a boy dashes from the car and passes her on the stairs even though in one hand he holds half a sandwich and in the other a clear baggie of cookies. He arrives at his grandmother and greets her face-first. He wipes his mouth on Annie's light-blue pants, then smiles up at me. "Hey!"

"Hey, yourself. I'm Jewel."

"Uh-uh—this is Mrs. Mantelle," Annie corrects him. "Markie, quit wiping your face on me. Thought I told y'all to stay in the car."

Leah is examining the crowded porch and then pulls off a sprig of jasmine. "Smell this, Grandma." She sticks it right up to Annie's face, where she bats it away like the branch is full of spiders.

"Leah, get that outta my face! Take Markie out there somewhere." She waves her hand at our big, wild yard, bordered by a tall, black, old-fashioned fence and big, old, rusty dumpster. "Give me one more minute."

She shoos them off the porch, then turns to watch them as she says, "By the time Aiden got to the station this morning, Mark, my ex-son-in-law, and his mother were there causing a scene. Apparently they'd called in first thing yesterday morning about Leslie being missing, but no one did anything. Guess it wasn't the first time she'd gone missing and the police had acted a fool about it." She swings her head back at me. "Is it okay if they climb on the fence?"

"Sure. I guess. So, how did they know she was missing if she doesn't live at home?"

Annie goes vague, waving a hand around and not looking at me. "Someone must've called them. I mean even if you don't want to see someone here, you can't help but see them. Know what I mean?"

I can't help but roll my eyes. "Okay. So I'm guessing the police didn't follow up?"

"Exactly. Aiden says the Callahans are fit to be tied and threatening to sue everybody and their brother. Of course soon as I heard I got the kids out of school. No need for them to have to hear what everybody will be saying. I was heading back to my house when I thought of you." Now she turns to face me completely. "Can you come help with the kids while I handle this new circus?"

"Sure, but…" I look down at my work clothes. "Can I change really quick?"

"Oh, absolutely! Don't worry, I'll be there most of the time, but in case I need to run out, you'll be okay with the kids." She sits on the wooden bench out on our porch and lifts her phone at me. "I have some calls to make, so no hurry on changing clothes. But if you hurry, that's okay too."

Attempting to ignore the complete mess the house is in, I scurry around getting ready. Having a friend ask for help feels strange. These ladies here don't pay a bit of attention to what I've always thought of as my hard shell. They just ignore it and trample on through. I laugh as I turn off the kitchen lights and grab my purse.

Whatever it is about this place, I kind of like it.

Annie's house sits way off the road behind a forest of pine and small palm trees. Her driveway is dirt and sand, and as we come out of the trees, the car is flooded with light. Past the house lays the marsh and the bright blue morning sky. Light reflects off the high water and the tin roof on the whitewashed house. It's a large, sprawling house with a porch wrapping all the way across the front. It's not new but not really what I think of as an old house. Ruts in the driveway make the car bounce, and the kids laugh as Annie revs up to give them more of a ride.

I hang on to the door handle.

"Annie, this is beautiful," I say between bounces.

"Thank you. Alan owned the land when I met him, and we lived here in a trailer when we got married. Building the house took a long time, but it turned out just like we imagined." She sighs as she puts the car in park. "Except for him not being here. Still hard to believe I've lived here more years without him than I did with him. It was twenty years ago this past February that he passed." The kids barely waited for the car to stop before they vaulted out of it. Annie and I sit and stare at the house for a moment. It looks like we'll need this moment of quiet, as people come spilling out the front door.

Annie points from where her hand rests on top of the steering wheel. "Here's that circus I was telling you about. That's my Amber. The one the kids ran up to." I watch the kids talk to the woman wearing a black shirt and pants, and it's easy to see she's not listening to them. She's talking over her shoulder at the man behind her. Shouting might be a better description.

The man is shouting back. He's a large guy wearing a dark-green T-shirt and a pair of well-worn jeans. He has on scuffed-up boots, and he's stomping one to apparently make a point. "Mark?" I ask.

"Yep. And right on cue, there's his momma. Eustis Callahan." The woman comes out the front door carrying a folded-up newspaper. She hits her son with it. She hits his arms, his legs, even his head.

"What is she doing?" I frown. "She's hitting him!"

"Yep. Don't do no good, but she tries. Watch. He'll just let her whale on him until he finally decides to shut his mouth."

We watch as the hitting stops, and Eustis talks to her son and Amber. They all turn to look at us.

Annie opens her car door and gets out. "Time to join the party." I reluctantly follow her lead and get out too. She winks at me over the top of the car. "Ready to meet the folks?"

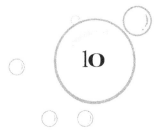

10

"Call me Eustis. We're right near the same age, so it's appropriate." The gruff little woman with strands of gray hair falling wildly out of her bun sticks out her hand to me—after throwing her folded newspaper off into Annie's flower bed.

"Hi. I'm Jewel." I reach out to shake her now-empty hand. "I'm so sorry for your loss."

Eustis looks confused, then recovers. "Oh yeah. That is a shame, isn't it?"

I then turn with my hand outstretched to her son.

He lights up and winks at me. "Why, hello there. Momma, there ain't no way in the world this young lady is anywhere near your age." As he leans close I can smell alcohol on his breath.

When he tries to hold my hand for longer than he needs to, Annie pulls me back and turns me to her daughter. "This here is my Amber."

Amber looks like her siblings in that she's attractive and has dark hair. She's heavier than the others and seems more serious. Of course, she has just found out that her ex's sister has been murdered, so that could be it.

Eustis turns from me and points at Annie. Eustis is small, but she has really long arms and her finger touches Annie's shirtfront. "You've got to talk to them, Annie. Get that boy of yours to talk some sense into 'em. They're acting like she was just with the wrong crowd, but she wasn't anymore." Now she actually pokes Annie's chest. "No, sirree. She changed back a couple years ago. Tell her, Mark."

Her son looks at the little woman and shrugs. "Sure, Momma. She changed. What d'ya want me to say? These cops here aren't going to give folks like us from off the island the time of day. They'll just shrug it off and say it's some county trash that was running with the wrong people." He throws up his hands. "I'm going back inside to get a drink."

Amber rolls her eyes. "Yeah, like that'll help," she says under her breath.

Eustis's pointed finger swings in her direction. "My boy needs a drink every so often seeing as he has to work sunup to sundown every day, him being a single father trying to run a farm all by his lonesome. He sure could use some help, but his wife has to live on this la-di-da island!"

Annie walks between them. "*I'm* gonna need a drink if you two start up again. Come on in, Jewel." She opens the front screen door for me to walk in.

I'm thinking I should've driven myself so I'd have a means of escape.

"Okay, okay," Annie finally says. "I'll go with you down to the station." As she stands up from her dining room table she asks me, "You're good with the kids?"

I'm leaning over the kitchen table in the next room, helping Leah glue cotton balls onto construction paper. I straighten and stretch my back. "Sure. We're good here. Although Markie has already finished his project." I shrug and grin as his grandmother had already gotten onto him about his slapdash manner concerning his project. He ignored her and moved out to the wide, screened-in porch to play with Legos and Oscar, the dog. Leah had explained to me that Oscar doesn't like yelling, so when everyone is excited, he stays on the porch. I don't think I knew that dogs paid that much attention to what humans do. Moving around my whole life has meant I've never owned a dog, so I've never really thought that much about them.

Eustis is standing in the front doorway, her purse over one arm and her other hand planted on her hip. "Come on, Annie!" she shouts. "Kids'll be fine."

Annie ignores her and comes to stand beside us; she meets my eyes and shakes her head. She strokes Leah's soft hair as the little girl concentrates on her gluing.

I nod towards the poster board. "Sea turtles. They seem to keep coming up."

"Aunt Leslie loves turtles. It was her idea," Leah says as she places one more cotton ball in place. "See? A nest! Then the mama covers it with sand and goes right back out into the ocean."

Annie hugs the little girl, who is busy rubbing glue off her fingers.

"You like it, Grandma?" Leah asks.

"Sure, sugar bug. Go wash your hands and then you can play with your brother."

As Leah runs off, Annie affectionately says, "God love 'em. They just roll with all this chaos. Shame what we put kids through, isn't it? Mark and Amber share time with them, but you can see they haven't worked through much of anything. That's why I don't really mind them spending so much time here with me." She rolls her eyes as Eustis growls from the living room. "I can't believe Mark went home and left his mother here for me to contend with."

I grin and agree with a nod. There's no need to say that her daughter left Annie holding the bag, too, what with *her* mother-in-law and *her* kids. Something about Amber having a house to show meant she had to leave. She and Mark were both gone within fifteen minutes of us getting here.

I whisper to Annie, "I hate to say it, but Eustis doesn't seem like a grieving mother."

"She's crazy as a bedbug, first of all," Annie whispers back, "but she also favors Mark. He's her golden boy. I'm not sure if Leslie has even lived with her for several years." She shrugs, then calls out to Leah and Markie, "Bye, kids! Y'all be good for Miss Jewel." Then she bustles out to where Eustis is sighing loudly and complaining even more loudly. I can see why Oscar stays on the porch.

"About time. Let's get this show on the road," the small woman says as she bangs through the screen door, leaving it to bounce in front of Annie. Annie pushes through, doing some of her own growling.

They squabble all the way to the car, but it's barely audible through the screen door.

"All clean!" Leah announces as she runs into the kitchen. "Can we go outside?"

"Sure." Peacefulness fills the space left by the loud, emotional people these little ones are related to. The screened porch out back runs the length of the house, just like the front porch. It's nothing fancy. The same terrazzo floor, a low ceiling of dark wood, and doors every so often leading down sets of wooden steps. The feel is more like a lodge at a summer camp than a house.

I follow both kids and their dog out one of the doors and down the steps, and ask if they want to put on shoes.

Markie turns to me. "We going somewhere in the car?"

"No! Definitely not going anywhere."

He shrugs. His hair is cut really short. It looks like a recent cut, as the skin around his ears and hairline is pale. "Don't need shoes if we're not going in the car." He takes off running before he finishes his sentence, as his sister had yelled, "Race you to the swing!" and blown past him. However Oscar beats them both.

A tire swing at the end of the house, hanging from the low limb of a large, looming tree, is their goal. They are both squeezed into it by the time I get there. Being with kids this age reminds me of why I wanted to be a teacher once upon a time.

They swing with only an occasional push from me, and I breathe in the air from the swamp, or marsh. I've been told its marsh, definitely not swamp. I don't know the difference, but it seems pretty important to people around here. There's a dock with a small boat tied to it. It's awfully quiet out here, but with all the birds going to and fro, it feels busy. Oscar races around the trees chasing squirrels, but the marsh birds seem to ignore him. He's a happy, shaggy dog, not too big, but definitely not small enough to fit in a purse like some of those actresses do with their dogs. His bark isn't even annoying or sharp. Come to think of it, I didn't hear him bark once while everyone was inside arguing and shouting. I bend to pet him as he comes near. Oscar is a pretty chill pup.

Markie jumps off the swing and heads to the other side of the tree where he pulls himself up onto one of its low limbs. I smile at Leah and see she's watching him as she hangs on her stomach in the tire swing. On top of the limb, Markie walks out toward the end, then settles into a sitting position. He gets the limb to bouncing like he's riding a horse.

"That's kind of neat," I say with a laugh as Oscar jumps underneath him like he's bouncing too.

Leah doesn't say anything. Then she blurts, "What happened to Aunt Leslie?"

"Oh, well…"

The little girl hangs her head and then kicks so the swing moves around. Still facing the ground she says, "I mean, I know she died. But where?" She looks up at me. "Grandma said she was at the beach. Did she drown?"

"They don't know. The police are trying to figure it out."

Leah kicks off harder, and the swing moves higher into the air. I step back toward the trunk of the tree. These poor kids already have so much to deal with, and now there's the death of their aunt.

Markie has left his pretend horse and walks the length of the limb back. He lies against the trunk and looks down at me, studying me. "I don't think she drowned.

She don't like the water. 'Member, Leah? She wouldn't ever go in the water, even when we all tried to get her to go in. Even when we were all in the water. She wouldn't come in."

"Do you like to swim, Miss Jewel?" Leah asks me, her sweet eyes all scrunched in concern.

"I'm not crazy about ocean water, but I do like to swim in a pool."

Leah pulls herself out of the swing. "Not me. I like the ocean. I'm like a sea turtle. I can swim a really, really long way!" Making swimming motions with her skinny arms, she heads toward the house. Of course, Oscar joins her, leaping and yipping.

Markie jumps out of the tree and leaps alongside them. "I'm a dolphin. I can beat a stupid old turtle any day!" With him jumping and her swishing, they run around the yard a bit, and then they climb the back steps. As they get to the top and open the screen door, they announce that it's time for lunch.

Only lunchtime? Feels like it's already been a full day.

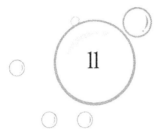

11

We're watching some cartoon about animals that save the earth when I hear Annie and Eustis walking up the front porch. Though I'm smushed between the arm of the couch and Leah, I maneuver without disturbing her from the show. Heading to the door, I can see Annie has her arm wrapped around Eustis's shoulders. I push open the door, and I smile at Annie. The look on her face surprises me. She looks shell-shocked. Her eyes keep blinking, and she's pale. I thought Eustis was crying, but her face mirrors Annie's. They come in past me, but I'm not sure they actually see me.

"What happened?" I ask. "The kids are watching TV. Can I get you something?"

Annie seems to come to. "Some water, please. Uh…" She looks around as if she's never seen this place. "Okay, let's go sit out back on the porch." She guides Eustis out one of the end doors where they won't be near the kids.

I grab bottles of water from the fridge and follow them out the door. They are seated on a nice set of rattan furniture with thick, burnt-orange cushions. I open the bottles, hand one to each of them, and then sit down.

Annie looks first at Eustis, who just stares at her water. Then Annie says in an almost whisper, "They arrested Mark for, the, for the murder."

"Mark? Amber's Mark?"

"My Mark!" Eustis declares with a glare at me. "My Mark. Who was at our house all night!"

"So he has an alibi. I'm sure they'll realize they made a mistake…" My words die off because Annie is staring at me, shaking her head.

Eustis frowns. "I can't understand it not being an alibi since he was there when I left and was there in the morning when I got up!"

Annie says, "Well, you did leave your house in the late afternoon."

"See! If he'd come to church with me like

he ought to, none of this would be a problem. They are just making things up. What do they think? That I raised animals?" She abruptly stands. "Annie, I'm going to go lie down on your guest bed for a bit. My head is about to pound itself right off my shoulders." She marches back into the house.

Annie takes a deep breath, then falls back into the thick cushions. "Poor Eustis," she says to me. "It was a nightmare. There we stand, waiting to speak to Aiden, when Detective Johnson comes prancing in with Mark in handcuffs. Mark is yelling and threatening everyone around him. When he saw his momma, he really starting yelling. 'I didn't do it, Momma. You know I didn't do it. Hell, I didn't even see her on the beach that night! You fix this, Momma. I'm counting on you!' All the way through the station until they got him back toward the jail."

"So he was on the beach Sunday night?"

Annie cocks one eyebrow at me. "You weren't the only one to catch that. He admitted to being at the scene of the crime."

"But I thought…" I lift my head to make sure the kids are still in the living room. "I thought it was kids on the beach. He's not a kid."

"No, not that he knows that. He's one of

those that always hangs around with younger people. Well, younger people that are partying." She shrugs and takes a sip of water. "He didn't so much when he and Amber were together, but once they separated, he went right back to it."

We stare out at the marsh, and then Annie leans forward, pats my knee, and says, "I bet you're ready to get home."

"I guess, but if you still need me, I can stay."

"Jewel, honey, you're a sweetheart. I was hoping this wouldn't explode into a bigger mess and it could stay quiet, but I should've known that if the Callahans were involved, there wasn't a chance of anything staying quiet. Sorry I dragged you into it."

"No, not at all. I'm kind of getting used to this having friends thing." I smile and reach out to pat her back as we stand. "And Leah and Markie are the cutest things ever." We look into the living room, where we can see them sprawled out on the couch and love seat.

"I do not want to have to tell them their daddy is in jail," Annie says with a huskier voice than usual.

"Do you think he did it?"

She takes a deep breath, and I can see her

thoughts bouncing around behind her eyes. Then with a small shake of her head she says, "Hiding a body in a turtle nest seems just crude enough for him. He's real fond of sick jokes, but he's never had a violent streak. He's almost too soft-hearted."

My head jerks back, and my eyebrows knit on their own to hear her say that.

She sighs and looks at me. "I know, I know. But just 'cause someone's a jerk, a flirt, and a drunk doesn't mean he can't be a weenie. Amber's actually the one trying to arrange his bail. She says there's no way he did it, and, well, she wants us ladies, the lunch group to, well, you know…" She swings her big, blue eyes at me. "We helped you and Craig."

"Oh, yes. That's true, but—"

A car door catches our attention, and we look through the house to the front windows. Annie pushes me forward. "There's Amber. Lucy, Cherry, and Tamela are waiting for us at Lucy's house."

While Amber fills her mother in on the bail situation, I step into the living room to say goodbye to the kids. "It was fun to hang out with you guys. I'm sure I'll see you again soon."

They move out of their TV trance long

enough to smile at me and say bye. Leah even jumps up to give me a quick hug. She's back in her spot on the couch before I can bend back up. I can't help but think how fun it'll be to have Carver visiting soon. Oh, my house. I hadn't thought about the mess I left there all afternoon, but it'll have to wait now.

We have another murder to solve.

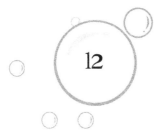

12

Lucy sets a platter of nachos down, then places her hands on her hips. "I'm sorry to say, but the general thought around the island is that Mark did it. I don't know what we're supposed to do about that."

"Not start off with our minds made up?" Tamela questions. "We solved Pierson Mantelle's murder, so of course we should look into this one. Annie's grandkids need us." Tamela is determined that we get involved, even more so than Annie, it seems. I'm not sure why. She smiles up at Lucy and says, "The nachos look amazing."

Our hostess sits down at the table, her back to the ocean. We're on the deck of her mother's beach house. "Mother hates onions," she says, "so I always love to have these when she's gone to her sister's."

"Where does her sister live?" I ask, lifting a spatula full of nachos and stringing melted cheese from the serving platter to my plate as I serve myself. The last time we were here, I fell in love in with Lucy's mother, Birdie. She made me feel so welcome with her charming smile and genuine interest in my story. While it was obvious how contented she is in her perch here beside the sea, she was more than ready to rush off and help us get answers about Pierson's murder. In a place like Sophia Island there are some things only the old-timers can get to the bottom of.

"St. Augustine Beach," Lucy says. "They visit back and forth a couple times a year. So what did Amber find out about the bail?"

Annie clicks her tongue as she holds up a loaded chip. "Nothing much. Amber can't stand having to ask her sister Abigale for help, but she did. Abigale was still working on it, trying to hurry things along when Amber left. She had to come home to take care of the kids."

Cherry grimaces. "Sounds like my girls, competitive to the end. Jo's moved back home, doesn't have a job, is cleaning my house for extra money, and her sister thinks she's living the life." She shrugs as she adds a jalapeño to the nacho in her hand. "But maybe this'll make Amber and Abigale closer. So Amber thinks there's no way her ex-husband did this?"

"No. She says he's basically a wimp. She says he and Leslie weren't close at all, that he couldn't care less what she might've been doing on the beach. Police said maybe he caught her misbehaving and got mad. Amber says no way. Has anyone heard how Leslie actually died?"

Cherry, our nurse, speaks up. "Asphyxiation is all I could figure out from what I heard at the hospital. I went back to check out the gossip. No head trauma or wounds. Not much to go on."

"She couldn't breathe?" Tamela says, a horrified look on her face. "From the sand?"

"No," Cherry shakes her head. "I can't imagine that. She had to have been dead when she was buried, right? She wasn't that deep."

"Maybe she drowned?" Annie says. "Could it have been an accident?" Her eyes light up. "Someone was scared they'd be blamed, so they—"

Lucy finishes for her. "They dug a hole, covered her up, and made it look like a nest?

No, I don't think this was any kind of an accident. Sounds to me like someone with a history with her." She doesn't say it, but we all hear "like her brother" in her words.

"Besides," I interject, "her niece and nephew said today that she didn't go in the ocean at all. She hated it. So if she drowned…"

"Then it wasn't an accident, but she's lived here all her life. Others had relationships with her outside her family, right?" Tamela takes a drink of water, then asks, "Was she close to Amber and Mark's children?"

Annie frowns. "A little bit, but I really don't know. Leslie was several years younger than Mark. I rarely saw his kids with her, but when they were at Mark's, who knows who took care of them? Eustis lets them kind of run wild."

Lucy scowls. "Like she did her own kids. The only time Mark kept his name out of the published police reports was when he was married to Amber." She takes a breath. "As for Leslie Callahan, she was just one of those girls that hangs out at the beach and gets into trouble."

"She in the police reports much?" I ask.

Lucy, Annie, and Tamela, who've lived here long enough to know, look at each other.

Lucy stands and picks up the nearly empty nacho platter. The beach wind ruffles her short, blonde hair and whips her peach silk shirt. "I think the trouble she got into was more in the boy trouble department. I seem to remember her being linked to a number of guys over the years." She pauses for a moment, thinking. "But I have to admit, I hadn't heard anything lately. Maybe she was trying to turn over a new leaf. Why don't you ladies clear these plates? I'll come back out and we'll have some more wine."

Annie is counting on her fingers as she stands up. "Okay. Amber is thirty-four, so that makes Mark thirty-eight. Leslie was between my two youngest, so she's around twenty-five. That's a big age difference for two kids."

Tamela reaches for my empty plate. "That's way too young to die. Poor thing. Also, poor mama to lose one child and have the other blamed for it." She sets down the plate she'd just picked up. "Y'all, I know I'm pushing this, but I feel so guilty, standing there over her all morning, fretting about a turtle." She looks toward the house, then whispers, "I think that's eating at Lucy too."

Annie shudders. "I'm so glad I wasn't there."

We all grow quiet as we collect the rest of the dishes. Annie and Tamela carry them inside, and Cherry and I move to stand along the railing. We look out at the ocean, where a half-moon is rising. The sun sets on the marina side of Sophia Island, which is about a mile behind us. Sunset on this side of the island is a gradual coloring of the sky over the ocean with streams of peach, blue, and purple. We watch people come and go on the beach below us. One fisherman is set up at the edge of the surf, and a couple walk behind their two toddlers, who have soaked their clothes by running from the waves.

The last shafts of sunlight come from behind us, then through the sea oats where there's a beach access and no house next door. A photographer has set up her equipment to photograph a young couple where the light meets the waves. The man is wearing khakis and a white shirt with his sleeves rolled up. His wife is wearing a long, light-colored dress. As the dress flattens against her, we can see that she's pregnant.

"I sure didn't want any pictures of me when I was pregnant," Cherry says with a bit of snark.

"Me neither. Of course, we didn't have the money to hire a professional photographer. Saved all that for baby pictures taken at the local department store."

The sunlight is perfect on the couple; it turns the cresting waves into gold. The wind picks up the woman's blonde hair, and the man laughs as he tries to corral it for her. They are seated on a beige blanket, and the photographer is having a field day, taking pictures from all angles. I imagine that these photos, the ones in which he's moving her hair and they're laughing together, will turn out to be the best ones of the bunch.

People think Florida is just full of old people, and I admit I'm enjoying being considered young, but there are so many families and couples like this one. I can't imagine any of my children leaving the Midwest, but maybe one day they will. Or at the very least they might consider a photo shoot on the beach.

"Refill?" we hear from behind us. Lucy, Annie, and Tamela are carrying their refilled glasses toward us, and Lucy is bringing the promised bottle.

"Just a little," Cherry and I say at the same time, and then Cherry waves her hand at the beach. "We're watching a photo shoot down there."

Leaning on the railing, Lucy explains

how this beach and this time of day are a favorite for photographers. Then she groans as she catches sight of the man being photographed. "That's Benjamin Perkins. He's been a royal pain in my backside. He moved here a minute ago and thinks he knows more about rescuing turtles than all of us put together."

"Oh, that's the guy?" Tamela leans over to get a better look. "He sure was acting all chummy with the councilmembers at the meeting last night."

"That's it!" I raise my glass to salute the jolt to my memory. "I kept thinking he looked familiar. He was wearing a suit, right?"

Lucy rolls her eyes. "He's a lawyer but wants to be a politician."

"Well, he married into the right family," Annie says with a laugh. "His wife is Amelia Little. Her father was a US senator, and her aunt is in the Florida House. Her uncle is something in the governor's office. I believe Amelia met Benjamin in law school in Georgia."

We watch as the photo shoot wraps up. The photographer heads toward the steps of the beach access while the couple stands, holding each other as they look out at the ocean.

After the ugliness we witnessed this week on the beach, this causes us all to relax so that we don't even notice when the couple finally walks away.

We stay as the sky darkens and a few stars appear to join the moon, which is quickly making its way higher. We turn and make our way back inside, Lucy turning on a few soft lamps while the rest of us collect our purses and check our phones.

My silenced phone leaps to life, and I see I have a string of missed calls. Annie glances at my phone. "Someone—is that Eden?—sure is trying to get a hold of you!"

"Yeah, I see that. Must be an emergency, she left a voicemail," I say with a small laugh as I push the voicemail icon and put the phone to my ear. We all share smiles because we know a twentysomething leaving a voice message means the world has probably already ended. I listen, struggling to keep my eyebrows from flattening and meeting in the middle. As soon as I hang up as I start for the door.

"I need to get home." My head is down and focused, but keeping my voice light, I say, "Thanks for dinner and the wine, Lucy." To their concerned questions, I turn, smile, and wave. "Oh sure, everything's fine. She just wants to ask me something."

I reach the door, and I'm off, running down the stairs to the parking area under the house. I maneuver around one of the house's supporting stilts, jump in my car, and am backing up, thankful I'm not blocked in. Whew. I did what Eden said, hard as it was.

"Come home now," she'd demanded. "And do not bring Annie with you!"

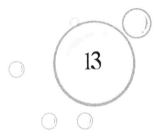

13

When I pull into our driveway, Eden stands from her seat on the top step of the porch. She meets me halfway down and hugs me tight. I'm barely getting used to hugs from my friends down here, so this hug feels too familiar. I push away like it's awkward for me to be standing on the steps. It *is* awkward, just not because of where I'm standing. "So what's going on?"

Eden's voice is lowered, and she's talking so quickly that it's hard to figure out what she's saying.

"Wait," I say. "Calm down. This girl is a friend of Leslie Callahan's? The girl that was, was on the beach? And she's here?" I lower my voice too. "Inside?"

Eden takes a deep breath and swallows a couple of times. We're still standing close to each other on the steps. "Yes. She kind of works with my mom and dad at their shop, Signs. So, I kind of, like, know her and we were in school together, but she's younger than me. She was with Leslie on Sunday, and now she doesn't know what to do."

"Have you told Aiden?"

Eden shakes her head quickly and bites her lip. "No. I told him I was sick tonight so he wouldn't come over here. She won't talk to him."

"So why did you want me to rush home?"

The young woman loops an arm through mine and pulls me up the steps, talking all the while. "We needed someone not from here, and you're, like, the only person I know that I trust who isn't from this area." At the door she pauses and meets my eyes for just a second. "Oh, and she needs a place to stay," she mumbles as she pushes through the door. "This is Sarah. Sarah, this is Miss Jewel. You can trust her."

The young woman on the low, velvet-covered settee is crying. Her quick look up at me shows puffy, red eyes and swipes of mascara where it's run down her cheeks. She's hunched in over her knees, which I can see through the splits in her jeans. These don't look like manufactured splits, like in fashion jeans; they look like the real deal, old jeans fraying at stress points. Frayed flip-flops and dirty hair complete the picture.

What in the world have I gotten myself into?

"Hi, Sarah." I start to sit in the chair across from her, but Eden prods me to sit next to the crying girl. Sarah doesn't look up as I sit. I reach out to pat her back, which brings on a deep sob and the words, "I just miss her so much."

I wrap my arm around her and pull her close as I realize this is the first true emotion I've seen for the dead girl. Leslie's mother and brother didn't seem genuinely upset. Even Annie and her daughter felt removed and distant about her.

Eden goes to the kitchen, then returns with glasses of water. "Here you go. Take a drink, sweetie."

Sarah sits back and gives me a quick, shaky smile. I take my glass and also sit back. She drinks, then uses the wadded-up tissue in her hand to wipe her nose and eyes again. "Sorry about that. It keeps hitting me every so often. This is your house?"

"Yes. Mine and my husband's. Are you from Sophia?"

"Yes, ma'am. Well, I am now. I was raised up in Georgia near the sub base. My daddy's in the navy."

"Oh, the submarine base. St. Mary's. I've hear of it. It's not that far, right?"

"No, ma'am, but my family doesn't live up there anymore. They moved back to Texas the year after I graduated. I wanted to stay here where my friends were. That's when I moved to the island."

"Oh." I look at Eden who's seated across from us. "Have you two been friends since then?"

Eden wrinkles her nose. "I'm not sure we ever thought of ourselves as friends, right, Sarah? We kind of run around in different crowds, but she works with my mom and dad some, so we know each other."

Sarah adds, "Plus I'm younger. Younger than everybody it seems, but I've always had older friends. Comes with growing up in the military."

She seems to be more settled, so I broach the subject of Leslie. "You were younger than Leslie, too, then, I guess?"

With a swallow, she nods, then tucks her

blonde hair behind her ear. "Yes, ma'am. We met in class. Out at the junior college."

"Leslie was in college? I haven't heard that before."

Sarah actually turns her body to face me. "Ma'am, no one was supposed to know about it. She lived on the down low." She squints. "You know what that means?"

"'On the down low'? Yes, I think so. She didn't want anyone to know, right?"

"Yes, ma'am, she—"

I stop her. "I understand and appreciate all the 'yes, ma'am' and 'no, ma'am,' but you've got to stop it. Please. I'm not from here, and it grates on my nerves. Just a simple yes or no will do."

Both young women blink at me. Sarah says, "Yes, ma—uh. Okay. I'll try."

Eden rolls her eyes at me, then turns to the younger girls "Tell her about Sunday."

"Okay." Sarah sets her glass down on the table beside her, tucks her hair back on both sides, and then buries her hands inside the long sleeves of her sweatshirt. "Leslie going to school was a secret because her father was paying for it. You see, no one knew she and her father were talking. They weren't supposed to even know about each other."

She untucks her hands, pulls another

tissue out of the pouch on the front of her hoodie, and wipes her nose again. "But he found her, oh, I don't know, a while back, and he wanted her to go to school real bad."

"Wait, what do you mean 'found her'?" I ask.

The girl shrugs. "That's just what Leslie said. She always wondered about him, she said. But then all of a sudden he found her."

"What about her mother?"

Sarah stares blankly at me, but Eden scoffs. "Eustis Callahan? She never had one bit of use for Leslie. Folks often wondered if she was really her granddaughter or a niece or something."

Nodding, I take a sip of water, then say, "That sounds about right from what I saw when I met her this afternoon. So what happened Sunday?"

Sarah's face slumps in and her eyes tear up. "We were drawing, over near the fort. That's what we'd do a lot."

"Drawing what?"

She frowns at me and shrugs. "Oh, everything."

Eden jumps in. "My bad. They're artists. That's how they met. I said she worked for my parents but didn't say how. Sarah draws artwork, tattoos for them."

Sarah smiles, and her shoulders lift. "Yeah, we're artists." Her face falls. "'Cept Leslie's not anymore." She covers her face with her hands and begins crying again.

She keeps talking through her tears, though. "She was having dinner with her father for the first time Sunday night. He was getting ready to introduce her to his family."

Eden looks at me with wide eyes, and mouths, "See?"

Yes, I see, but I don't see what they think I can do about it. "Sarah, you have to tell the police."

"But I don't know anything else," she exclaims, looking up at me. "We finished drawing because I had to get ready for work. I went back to the room to change, and she went to the beach for a bit. She didn't have to get ready for her dinner until later."

"Where do you work?"

She sniffles and laughs. "Where don't I work? I wait tables wherever I can get some hours, especially in the off season. Sunday I was at Café Mango for a special event upstairs."

"And?" I prompt her, but she just stares down at her hands.

Finally she looks up with a sigh, staring

across the room at nothing. "I didn't see her again."

"When did you know she was missing?" I ask.

"I didn't really. I went out and had a drink or two after work, and it was late when I got in. I noticed she wasn't around, but…" She finishes with another shrug.

"Around? Around where? "Where would you have seen Leslie that late? Were you roommates?" I look to Eden for clarification, but she gets up and walks around the room, seemingly ignoring me.

Finally she says from near the stairs, "Tell her. We've got to tell someone."

Sarah spills. "Leslie had a room in a house up in The Settlement. They're not supposed to rent rooms up there because it's some historical thing, but, well…" She frowns and stops talking. Her lips shut, rub against each other. Neither woman says anything, but the tension in the room rises. Could there possibly be more tension over an apartment than a murder?

"Why is this such a secret? I don't get it."

Eden slumps back down into her chair. "Everybody knows it, but we're not supposed to talk about it. I guess it's illegal, you know? Say the owner can't sell the house or it needs renovation, but instead of letting it sitting empty, they rent out a room or two. Everybody just looks the other way."

"There's plenty of parking up there so we just spread our cars out and move them often, and no one notices, like in a neighborhood." Sarah lifts her hands. "I used to rent a room way out near the interstate, but it's boring out there and so far from work. Leslie let me share her room, and that meant we had more time for our art. We didn't have to work so many shifts because it was so cheap."

"But who owns the house?"

Eden sighs, then says, "Houses. There are three of them."

"All in this same area? Uh, settlement?"

Sarah giggles and holds up a hand, and the conversation. "*The* Settlement. You have to say the '*The*'. All the old people up there are hyped up on the '*the*' part."

"Okay." Gosh, I hate talking to young people sometimes. I mean, we are talking about a murder here. "*The* Settlement. Who owns them?"

The giggling dies down, and the girls stare at each other. Finally Eden looks at me and with widened eyes says, "Amber Bryant."

Oh. Okay. Guess I see the problem now.

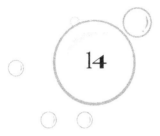

14

I didn't sleep a wink.

I may never sleep again. I've lost count of how many cups of coffee I've had sitting here in my kitchen nook, looking out the window. Well, out as far as the jasmine vines scaling the house and the wild bushes will let me. My eyes are fixed on a spot of dark red. It's Sarah's car. After Sarah told me she and Leslie were squatting—although is it squatting if the owner is renting you the squatting space?—in my friend's daughter's property, she then said that when she heard Leslie had been killed, she'd cleaned out their room. Then she'd driven around, not sure of what to do when she saw Eden walking near my house.

And now all of Leslie Callahan's possessions are sitting in my driveway.

Think the police might want to know that?

Unburdened, the girls went up to bed. Yes, of course I let Sarah stay here. Why not keep everything in one place so the police don't have to look so far? And we are calling the police first thing this morning whether the girls want to or not. My phone rings—my daughter Erin. I knew she'd want more details after what I dumped on her yesterday. I hit the green button and hear her say, "Hi. You're up early. It's not even six there."

"It's a 'going into the office' day for me," she says. "So, what is really going on with you and Dad? I kind of understood when he didn't want to retire, but you say he's basically living at the jobsite? How far away is that from you anyway?"

"About seven hours. He hates this house, and there is a lot of it to hate. He also hates the town and the island."

"But you? Do you hate it all too?" Erin sounds worried, and that's not good for a pregnant woman.

I push out a laugh. "I actually am loving the island and the town. You'll see when you come." The coffee seems to help me talk, fast and loose. "I've got someone helping me with the house, and I bet when your dad sees it he'll change his mind and be ready to retire."

Look at that—coffee's helping me lie too.

I hear the honk of a car horn, and Erin mutters under her breath.

"Erin Michelle, are you driving while you're on the phone?"

"Mom, it's the only way I have time to talk to you today. I'm fine."

"Well, I'm fine here also, so we can hang up. Don't worry about me and your dad. You just take care of yourself and our grandchild."

"Okay, I'm pulling into the garage, so I'll lose you anyway. Love you. Have a fun day!"

"Yeah, you too," I say with a huge roll of my eyes and a tiny shake of my head as I hang up. "*So* much fun to have today."

A knock at the front door surprises me, though I'm not that surprised when I see the blue of an officer's uniform through the front window. Of course Aiden couldn't stay away. Pulling and pushing, I get the door open. When I do, I am back in the surprised column to see which officer it is. "Officer Greyson. Good morning."

"Mrs. Mantelle, I remembered you get up early, and I wanted to check on something."

Officer Greyson is Aiden Bryant's older

partner. He was smart and kind during the investigation of my husband, and he actually feels like a friend. We'll see how much longer that lasts when he finds out who's upstairs. "Oh, well, I am up. What do you want to check on?" I step out onto the porch and pull the door closed behind me. Thankfully I'd put on jeans and a T-shirt earlier.

He looks to the side of my house and raises his eyebrows. "Isn't that Sarah Benoit's car in your driveway?"

I walk past him to the edge of the porch, then bend to look over the railing. Even as I'm doing it I'm thinking it's stupid. Am I going to act like I don't know the car is there? "Oh yeah. I guess so." Leaning against the railing, I fold my arms across my chest and smile at him. I try to act calm, but the coffee is no longer helping.

He smiles back. "Do you think I can talk to her? I'm assuming she's here. Or do you want to go see about that too?"

"She's asleep," I admit. "She's a friend of Eden. You know Eden, right? Um, Eden Carstons? Yeah, that's it."

He sighs, a sigh so big his chest, his thick utility belt, and all the patches on his shirt lift, then fall. Before he can get out the words that were going to follow that sigh, there are footsteps coming down the stairs in the house.

Officer Greyson turns to the door and gives it a slight push. "Good morning, ladies."

Eden is thin with short, dark red hair. Sarah is much shorter and stockier, with dusky skin and long, blonde hair. It looks much blonder now that it's clean, so blonde that I realize it's bleached. Her eyebrows are dark brown, and I bet her hair is actually closer to that color.

Sarah has on her clothes from last night, the ripped jeans and the hoodie. Eden is wearing pajama pants and a thin tank top. She's so busy protecting her friend that she doesn't seem to notice the show she's providing her boyfriend's partner. "Does Aiden know you're here?" she says, arms planted on her hips.

"No. Officer Bryant is looking for Miss Benoit elsewhere. That is your car, Miss Benoit, right?" he asks with a cocked eyebrow and a tip of his head toward the driveway.

"Yes, sir," she barely whispers.

"You were seen with Miss Leslie Callahan Sunday afternoon. You two were friends?"

Tears fill her eyes, and all Sarah does is nod as Eden wraps her arms around her. As

Sarah starts crying harder, Eden whispers in her ear and rocks her gently.

We all stand and wait, but the crying gets harder. Officer Greyson takes a step away from the door and back in my direction. He turns so he can see us all. "Why don't I let you ladies get dressed and composed. I'll come back in say thirty minutes to talk. We just need to wrap up some loose ends."

Eden smiles and says, "Thank you." She and Sarah turn back into the house.

Greyson walks past me and is halfway down the steps when I say, "Is that all? Loose ends?"

He stops and turns back to me, then lets out a groan before he says, "We've been told in no uncertain terms that this is a closed case." He simply stands there staring at me.

"And?" I say. There's got to be more.

He shrugs. "And nothing. We have a suspect who says he was there, who has a long history with the department, and who had a motive." As if he can't help himself he adds quietly, "Apparently."

"So what was his motive?" I step out from behind the railing and down one step. "I assume we're talking about Mark Callahan?"

He just barely nods. "I'll be back in thirty minutes," he says, but he remains still.

I try again. "So what was his motive? If he thought maybe he was protecting her? Maybe she got in the way? That could be accidental, right? Is that what you're calling a motive?"

"For him to be protecting his sister, it seems like there'd need to be a third party involved. We can't find a third party, so…" He smirks. "All I know is it's a closed case from on top." He leans toward me and mutters, "Way, way on top." Straightening up he says, "I'll be back." Then he jogs down the steps and out to his car.

Huh. Am I just imagining that he's telling me to look into the girl's death? Actually encouraging me and the lunch bunch to snoop?

What kind of rabbit hole have I fallen down?

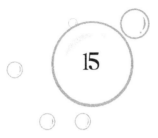

15

"Amber changed her mind. She's not paying his bail, and she pulled Abigale off the case." Tamela is short, but powered with righteous indignation. I'm having trouble keeping up with her as we walk the beach. "Mark Callahan did not murder his sister, but everyone is just throwing him to the wolves," she snarls. "Annie included!"

When I found out Sarah wasn't going to tell Officer Greyson the truth, I decided to not be anywhere near my house for the interview. She's determined to not fill him in on Leslie's secret father or her dinner plans with him. That feels a bit too much like hiding evidence for me, so I decided to check in on things elsewhere.

Tracking down Tamela during her morning walk wasn't hard. She parks in the same place, walks in the same direction, turns at the same place, and wears her green turtle shirt every morning. However, this has not been the peaceful stroll I expected. She's railed on about the murder investigation the whole time we've walked, going over and over how suddenly everyone pulled back and now Mark is guilty.

"I still don't understand why you are so sure he's not guilty," I say again. "*He* doesn't even act that sure of it. He doesn't remember being on that part of the beach, but he doesn't remember much else either." I wipe my face with the tail of my shirt. "Sounds like he was too drunk to know exactly what he did."

"So, for that, just railroad him right into a jail cell?" She presses her lips and shakes her head before suddenly stopping and turning to me. "It's up to us. He needs us, just like Craig needed us."

"But Craig was innocent," I protest. "Besides, the police have closed the case."

She squints at me. "How do you know that?" She starts walking again. "Oh, Aiden."

"Nope."

That slows her down. "Oh, Officer

Greyson, I bet." She stops walking. "He likes you. When did you talk to him?"

"He doesn't like me. He came by the house because…" Oops. "Let's keep walking. It's getting hot out here." I move to walk closer to the water. "The friend Leslie was with on Sunday is also a friend of Eden, and she stayed at my house last night. The police want to talk to her to quote, 'Wrap up some loose ends.' They've been told the case is closed from on top. Officer Greyson added, 'Way, way on top.'"

We've slowed and are only strolling now. Tamela is watching her feet as she thinks. "Could that be about the shrimp festival coming up? I know this is a small town and all, but are we really that shallow? Are we really that shallow to rush closed a murder investigation so it doesn't slow down the party?"

At the beach access where we'd parked, Tamela and I climb the steps and walk along the boardwalk. Skirting the tops of the dunes, we look down to see vines and flowering plants holding the dunes in place. Ahead of us houses awaken, a few with people on the decks enjoying coffee. Sophia Island has a limit of forty feet in height for beachfront property. Along with the many beach accesses, it helps the island feel more like an old-fashioned seaside town.

"I'm going to tell you everything," I decide. "Since the girl, Sarah, is not going to tell the police, I need someone else to talk this over with."

Tamela nods but doesn't say anything else as I fill her in on what Sarah said about Leslie's father.

"She said he's well known on the island?" Tamela asks.

"Exactly." I raise my eyebrows. "What if he's the reason this is a closed case? What if he doesn't want the police looking into this anymore?"

"But it doesn't sound like he would've wanted to kill her if he was getting ready to introduce her to his family," she says as we reach our cars.

"No. That's true. I don't know. I want to get back to the house before Eden leaves for work, see what Sarah told the police. I'll talk to you later."

"Yep." Tamela turns back to me as she has a sudden thought. "Oh, and so why did this girl, Sarah, spend the night at your house last night? Where does she live?"

I laugh and with the press of a button unlock my car door. "Oh, that's another story you've got to hear." Still laughing, I get in, start the engine, and wave as she gets in her car. The air conditioning feels heavenly. I sit and enjoy it for a moment, thinking about Sarah and Leslie's accommodations up in The Settlement.

Wait...

I wonder if Annie knows about Amber's houses in The Settlement. It's definitely something to check out.

Even though I've cooled off from our walk, I'm still sticky and can't wait for a quick shower. However, pulling into the driveway tells me that I'll be talking to Annie sooner rather than later and that my shower is on hold. Annie's car is parked there, but Sarah's is gone. There's no police car either, so that's a good thing.

As I climb the front steps, I try to see who is in the living room, but the windows only show me a reflection of myself. Opening the door, I say, "Hello?"

Annie comes from behind the door and pulls it open. "I can't find a thermostat in this place. Please tell me that tiny window air conditioner in the kitchen isn't the only way to cool this house?"

"Okay, I won't tell you, and I know, we're going to die this summer."

"You've got that right, sister! You have to remedy this immediately."

"I'm working on it." I push past her into the kitchen and get a big glass of ice water. "Has Eden left for work already?"

"Yes. Sarah took her."

"So you met Sarah?"

Annie sighs and slumps into one of the chairs at the kitchen table. "This is all such a mess. You've got to help me figure it out. Amber cannot lose her real estate license! Just cannot!"

"Is that why she's no longer putting up her ex-husband's bail and why she's no longer paying for his lawyer?"

Annie's chin is practically resting on her chest, but her big, blue eyes look up at me. "So you heard all that?"

"Yes. Is it because she thinks he's guilty or because she doesn't want anyone looking into The Settlement?"

"Ouch," she says. "That makes it sound so bad." So she does know about The Settlement. Well, that's one of my questions answered. Chin sinking even lower, if possible, Annie mumbles, "I don't know."

"Were you here when Officer Greyson came back to talk to Sarah?" I ask.

"Kind of. I saw him pull in, and so I parked around the corner. He was only here a couple minutes because the girls left before he got here. I'd texted Eden I was coming over, and she told me they were leaving quick. I talked to the girls around the corner, where I was parked. They pulled up next to me after Charlie found no one home. Then I came here."

"Where did Sarah go?" I ask as I untie my walking shoes. I forgot to leave them outside, and I've tracked in a dune full of sand. I wait for her answer, but then I realize she's not giving me one. "Annie? Where did Sarah go? The police are really going to want to talk to her now."

Barking from the back of the house gets our attention. "Oh, Oscar!" Annie says as she jumps up. "Squirrels are probably messing with him. Oscar, shush!"

I follow her down the back hall, and she continues yelling at the dog, the one that's apparently in my backyard, the entire way. She opens the back door, and Oscar immediately forgets the squirrels chattering at him from the tree limbs. He radiates pure joy. And produces more barking.

"See, this is why I can't have a dog. I completely forgot I left him out here," she says as she goes to him, untangling his leash from around a small tree. She's soon distracted by her ringing phone.

Amber's dog and I had bonded at Annie's house yesterday, so I greet him with a hug and a massage of his ears while Annie answers her phone.

Annie wanders around the yard on her call, makes her way back over to us, and then hangs up. "That was Lucy. She is beside herself. Remember that woman from the other day at the fake nest, the mean one? Sheila Hornet's Nest or Hornsby or something. Anyway, she's filed a complaint about Turtle Trackers and has started her own turtle group."

"Oh man. Lucy has got to be livid." Oscar shows he's concerned by sitting between us, actively following our conversation. I reach down and scratch behind his ears. "See, even Oscar knows that's a bad idea."

"Oscar? Yeah right," Annie says with a smirk at our four-legged friend. "Listen, what I need to know is if Charlie, you know, Officer Greyson knew where Sarah was living. You know, about The Settlement houses."

"He didn't appear to, but who knows?

Could Amber seriously lose her license over that? Why was she doing it?" I reach down and pick up a stick. Straightening up, I throw it and watch Oscar chase it. Annie is reading her phone, or ignoring my question, so I try again. "I guess I don't get what the big deal is. Are you worried about it?"

"Of course I'm worried!" she snaps. Then she frowns at me. "Honestly I'm not supposed to know how far it's gone. It may seem I'm all up in my kids' business, but I know they need to think I don't know everything. Heck, sometimes I wish I didn't know as much as I do! Only way to live peaceably so close to family is to ignore what they want you to ignore."

"I can see that. I can also see how hard that must be."

This time Annie picks up the stick Oscar drops at our feet. She throws it as she says, "It started out with her brothers and sisters and even some of their friends living up there from time to time, especially when the housing market here stunk. With all the historic designation stuff, it was impossible to sell the houses because renovations would be out-of-this-world expensive. Then, over time, everybody kind of forgot about it except other young people who needed a cheap place to live near their jobs on the island. I intentionally haven't thought about it in forever, but now..." She shrugs again.

I move to the steps to sit down. "And where's Eustis? Did she go back home? I can't imagine planning my child's funeral."

Annie motions for me to scoot over. "Eustis had a hissy fit at Amber last night when she took back paying Mark's bail. They were in the middle of it when I got home from Lucy's." She sets her elbows on her knees. "Eustis said she'd take care of it all herself and hightailed it out of my driveway. I haven't heard anything more since then." As she's talking she gets a text and swipes her phone open to read it.

"Oh my word! It's from Amber. Eustis is holding a press conference at the jail at noon today."

"For what?" I ask as Oscar runs over to get in on the excitement.

"Amber doesn't know yet but will let me know." She stands up and says to the dog, "Okay, boy. Let's go see your momma and find out what your crazy grandma is up to." When I laugh she corrects herself, "Your *other* crazy grandma."

I'm still sitting and thinking as they start around the house, so I jump up to catch up with them. "Hey, Annie. With such a big age difference between Mark and Leslie, has anyone ever talked about them having different fathers?"

She stops and turns to me, staring for a minute. Then she turns back around and keeps moving toward the car, opening the door for Oscar to jump in. She stands in the open door and looks back at me again. "Yeah, there was talk, but Mark's daddy was a mean ol' son of a gun, so no one questioned it out loud. He was as ornery as his son is wimpy. He died right before Amber and Mark got married. Why?"

"Just wondering. Let me know if you hear anything else."

She gets in the car, pushing Oscar out of her seat, and leaves. I run up the back steps to get a shower before anything else can happen.

The house feels too quiet.

Maybe I should get a dog.

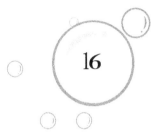

16

"Of course I want Leslie's killer found! What kind of idiot question is that? What do you people think I'm doing here in the first place?" Eustis is practically spitting at the handful of reporters in front of her.

There's a group of us gathered around a TV on the outdoor decking at The Tide. Situated across the local highway, A1A, from the beach and some condos, The Tide has been around longer than the resorts. Most of its seating is on multilevel decks in front of an old motel. I don't think you can still rent a room here, but maybe you can. Lucy lives not far from here, and apparently The Tide is her home away from home, where her Turtle Tracker friends hang out. They've called another emergency meeting, this time just for them, but the meeting had to stop to watch the press conference.

One of the bartenders laughs out loud at the TV and says again, "That old lady is a riot!"

Lucy frowns at him, but then she looks at me and her shoulders drop. We share a slight grimace before we look back at the TV.

"What have the police told you about their investigation?" a reporter yells.

"That it's closed!" Eustis yells back. "Aren't you listening?" She runs a hand through her hair, which is already sticking up from sweat and frustration. "They've got their man, and it's my son, Mark, but he didn't do it! I just need y'all to ask people to call me if they saw anything on the beach Sunday night. Or, hell, call the police." She sweeps an arm around her. "Or call one of these news stations. My son is not a murderer. Leslie was just in the wrong place at the wrong time." The camera pans in close as for the first time she shows an emotion other than anger. Her eyes fill with tears, and her bottom lip shakes. "I thought she'd changed, but she hadn't. Figures something like this would happen."

Our group groans as the reporters jump all over that.

A woman seated in front of me pushes back from the bar and stands up. "Throwing her own daughter, her own dead daughter, under the bus! I can't watch any more of this."

She moves off, and Lucy motions for me to take the open seat next to her own. She calls out to the woman, "Dawn, we'll continue the meeting in a bit." She then leans over to me and whispers, "I hear you're investigating? Tamela says the police asked you to?"

"What? No. Tamela is exaggerating."

The people around us groan again, so I go back to listening. Eustis looks helpless now, confused even, but she keeps talking. "She hung out at the beach all the time. She left home to live over on the island a couple years ago. Lots of kids in beach towns do that from what I hear." She shakes her head and looks down. "She and I never did get along…" Just as she has everyone on her side, her head flips up and she glares at the closest reporter. "Not like my son. He's a good man trying hard to raise his children. Leslie was just a lost cause, but they can't take my son away! He was only at the beach to be with friends and relax from a long week of work. He didn't murder nobody! Much less his sister!"

This time I have to agree with the woman

that left. "Lucy, this is awful. I don't think I can watch anymore." On the screen, Eustis throws up her hands, turns, and walks away. There's a bit of a cheer as the bartender quickly presses the mute button.

Lucy stands up on the lower rung of her barstool so she can be heard and seen. "Turtle Trackers? Our meeting continues in ten minutes back at our table." She sits down and leans closer to me. "Thanks for coming all the way out here. I've got to get ahead of this disaster with the turtles, but I want to be kept up to date on what you find out. Let me know what kind of help you need."

Lucy works for the city or the chamber of commerce or something like that, so she knows everything and everybody. She's an avid tennis player and in charge of the local tennis club. She's lived here her whole life and her boyfriend is one of the owners of one of the resorts, so she has connections there too. In short, she's my ticket to information; now, if I only had any idea at all what I need to know. I'm discovering I might need to be nosier than I naturally am to be a detective. Plus, I only just started reading mysteries, so I'm not sure I'm the best choice to be doing this.

I open my mouth, but then I shut it. Finally, I blurt out to her, "I don't know. I do think someone high up is closing the investigation, pinning it on Mark. I think Officer Greyson thinks that too. Tamela seems way too invested in Mark not being guilty while Annie seems to not care." My foot is tapping fast on the bar rail, and my words are keeping time with the speedy taps. "Annie is more worried about Amber losing her real estate license because of the—oh, oh, never mind." Lucy's blue eyes skewer me, but I push on. "Leslie's father. Have you ever heard that she and Mark don't have the same father?"

Now her eyes lose focus as she stares past me in thought. "Leslie Callahan. Eustis Callahan. Hmmm." When someone from the meeting area calls her name, she looks that way but says to me, "No. Mark Senior was her father; I'd bet on it. Listen, I've got to get over there." She jumps off her stool, but I grab her arm.

"Don't make that bet. He wasn't her father. Just before she was murdered, Leslie had met her father, and he was someone important on the island."

Lucy pats my hand with a shake of her head. "I'm not so sure about that. Something like that would have been gossiped about, and I would have heard it at some point. People think they have secrets, but they usually don't. I have to go. Thanks again for coming out this way, honey!"

The dozen or so people around the Turtle Trackers' table envelop Lucy, and she holds up a hand to get some order. I turn back to the muted TV and see it's time for the weather. They're calling for beautiful, temperate days all week, which apparently April is known for here. There's no surprise like the April snow showers up north. When I send the kids pictures of the beach or say I've been eating outside already, they find it hard to believe. Smiling, I turn away from the bar and step down. They'll all get to see Sophia Island for themselves soon, I think, but then there goes my smile. Soon—as in six weeks or so. I've got a house to fix, not to mention my marriage, before they get here. At the very least I need to start writing a to-do list.

"Not having lunch?" the bartender asks before I take even a step away.

"No," I say, looking over my shoulder, but then I get a glimpse of the ocean across the highway and a waitress delivering a tray of food to a nearby table, baskets of fried shrimp with a side of slaw and hush puppies. I can smell the oniony seasonings and hot, fried cornbread from here. I can turn away a bread basket any day, but since moving here I've discovered an almost mystical connection with hot hush puppies.

Besides, I can write a list sitting at a bar watching the ocean, right?

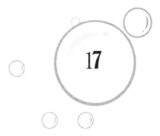

17

"I'm exhausted," Eden says as she flops onto the velvet love seat. "But look at this place."

Already half lying on my new—well, new to me—lounging couch, I raise my head to look around. "It looks so much better. I owe your dad for all those trips to Barnabas."

She grins. "He's a good one, but honestly he doesn't mind. He volunteers there all the time anyway. His men's group at church does a lot of work for them too."

Eden's pile of our furniture and other things to be donated is gone. Her father, Ted, had loaded up the back of his small pickup truck three times and hauled it all to an island charity called Barnabas. The resale shop at Barnabas is always jumping and provides support for their many ministries with needy families in the area.

The items we plan on keeping or selling have been relegated to an unused room behind the kitchen. It was already being used for storage, but Eden straightened it up, sorted it into items to donate or throw away, and turned it into an orderly storage area. I want to eventually use it as a bedroom for when we have company, so she's getting us set up on Facebook Marketplace and eBay.

With a groan, Eden sits up, her elbows on her knees. "I need to get in the shower. Aiden gets off at seven."

"What time is it?" I ask, and she holds up her phone to show me. "Six thirty? No wonder I'm starving. After my lunch at The Tide I thought I would skip dinner, but we've worked hard."

"Come with us. We're going to The Circle. They have killer hamburgers and lots of other stuff. His family gets together there on Tuesdays, but since last night was so crazy and there's no church tonight, they're doing it tonight."

"Oh, it's family." I wave her off. "I'll fix something here. Besides, I might be too tired to go out." I laugh and lay my head back. "I can't believe this was in the storage room. I've always wanted a lounging couch like this." The brown leather chair has a high back, wide arms, and stretches out to accommodate my long legs nicely.

"It's not an antique, but it's a very nice piece of furniture. Honestly, it doesn't seem like it belongs with the rest of Cora's things, but it looks good in here." Eden gets a text as she's talking. "Okay, it's all good. You're invited to come. No, you are *implored* to come to dinner." With a laugh she reads another text, then looks at me, shaking her head. "Miss Annie says, 'Tell her to not make me come get her, because I will,' followed by a half-dozen exclamation points."

She gets up, a second wind hitting her. "I'm getting in the shower, which is going to feel amazing. Aiden can drive us both." She's almost to the top of the stairs by the time she finishes talking.

"I'll just wait here for my own second wind," I mutter. Eden has gotten more done in my house already than I have in the almost three months I've lived here. Of course I helped, but she made those decisions I've been struggling with. Her knowledge of furniture is formidable. Her father was helpful in not only moving things but in suggestions for laying out the furniture. He said that he was over everything that needed to be done to move their tattoo shop and sell their home and that he was glad to be working somewhere else today. Eden said her mom was glad her dad was somewhere else today, too. Shoot, I barely live with my husband; I can't imagine working with him every day.

My new chair is situated so that I can see the front porch and lawn from it as well as the television once we get it hooked back up. Right now it's sitting on an old coffee table against the wall to my right, but Eden is on the lookout for an antique, or antique-looking, cabinet so that we can close the doors and hide it. The settee, which I didn't think I'd like, is perfect at an angle, with its back to the front door. "It defines the parameters of the room," Ted had said.

A chimney sweep is just one of the many people I need to call starting tomorrow. Ted believes the fireplaces in the Mantelle house are all functional, and if that's the case, then that will dictate how the rest of the furniture is placed. Swinging my legs off my chair, I sit up and unbend slowly to stand. Maybe going out to eat isn't such a good idea. I slept very little last night, walked the beach with Tamela this morning, and then worked all afternoon.

I'll see how I feel after a shower—if I can stay awake through it.

Loud voices from downstairs greet me when I turn off the water in my shower. Quickly I put on my robe and pull open the bedroom door to listen.

"Of course I called him!" I hear Aiden shout. "You've avoided us all day. Even skipped an appointment this morning."

Eden implores, "Sarah, just stay and talk to him. He's really a nice old guy."

I shut the door and quickly get dressed. I'm pretty sure the old guy is Officer Greyson, and I don't want to miss their talk. My stomach growls, and I hope their talk goes by quickly—after I get down there, of course. I dry my hair just a bit, then pull it back in a ponytail. One thing about living in a beach town: there's always someone that looks like they just came in off the sand. You've heard the phrase "Beach hair, don't care"? Well, it's true.

With my sandals in hand, I hurry down the stairs. "What's going on?"

Sarah is sitting on the settee with Eden. Aiden is at his post beside the front door, and his partner is sitting on the bottom of my chair. Hmm, I guess I'll let him have it for now.

I choose a chair on the other side of the settee. Officer Greyson nods at me, and Sarah gives me a shaky smile. She's holding a sketchpad across her knees, and she's crying softly. Eden catches my eye and mouths, "She told them everything."

Shoot, I missed it.

"So, no idea who she claimed her father was? Just someone important?" Greyson asks.

"No, and I don't think she said he was important. She said he was well known." Sarah works her mouth back and forth as she thinks. "Or maybe she did say important. She was really happy about it. I don't think she liked her other dad much."

"And he wanted to help her? Paid for classes and such?"

"Yep. He'd decided to introduce her to his family. Sunday."

It's obvious that this makes Officer Greyson nervous. He stares at his notes, then says, "Yeah, that's what you said. But you don't know where or exactly when or any details?"

She nods. "Yeah, at his house. On the beach."

We all look at her, and as she notices, she

asks Eden, "Didn't I tell you that?" She adds a shrug. "But it doesn't really matter. I mean, there's hundreds of houses on the beach."

Aiden has come over to stand closer to the young women. "But those kind of details gives your story some credence. Think, Sarah. What else do you remember?" He kneels down so he's looking right at her, and she lifts her eyes toward him and smiles.

"You look so grown-up and official," she says with a giggle, and I watch Eden bristle.

Sarah widens her eyes, gasps, and then asks, "Would it help if you had Leslie's sketchpads? Maybe she drew pictures of him." As if she'd set off an air horn, everyone in the room jumps a bit. Pictures of the poor girl's unknown father? If he's well known, then folks will probably recognize him. Just like that, the secret could be figured out. Aiden and his partner both stand. Eden frowns, and I hurriedly slip on my sandals.

"Yes, we do need to look through her things," Aiden says, remembering halfway through his sentence to soften his voice and smile.

"Sure, Aiden. It's all in my car. I packed up everything from your sister's place in The Settlement. I bet she's pretty angry I ran out on the room, isn't she? I don't know how much Leslie was paying her."

Aiden looks at his partner, turns red, then bustles to the front door, saying loudly, "Don't worry about all that. Let's go take a look in your car." He checks behind him. "Right, Charlie?"

Officer Greyson pulls on his hat as he plows past Aiden. "Let's get this done."

I don't think anyone on Sophia Island wants to talk about The Settlement or Amber Bryant's houses.

The three of them are gone when Eden releases a growl. She jumps to her feet, and, hands on her hips, she throws out, "Should we even wait to ride with him to go to supper? If Aiden and Sarah want to flirt, there's no need for me to stick around and watch. Can you drive?"

Her anger makes me smile, which I try to hide. It's easy to be laid-back in a relationship—right up until someone else wants your guy. "But maybe we should stay with Sarah?" I suggest. "See what they find?"

Eden's jaw is tight and jutting out. "They won't tell us anything. Let's go eat." She heads out the front door and across the porch. I follow her, though I slow down as I walk near Sarah's car. She's sitting in the passenger's seat, and Aiden is in the driver's seat. Their heads are together, gathering things from the back seat while Greyson is looking over the loaded trunk.

He steps toward me and turns so his back is to the others. "Miss Mantelle, you weren't here either this morning when I came back."

"No, I was, uh… Yes, I wasn't here."

"Did you see Mrs. Callahan's press conference?" He raises his eyebrows and shoots me a quick grin.

"Yes." I lower my voice. "Do the higher-ups still think Mark killed his sister?"

He barely nods, and all traces of a grin die. "He admits he was on the beach, and, well, he isn't helping himself. He says after his mother is gone his sister would have inherited half the farm and would probably have forced him to sell it. He said she was unreasonable to deal with. Shouted it, actually. And said that she didn't deserve half as she'd never worked one day on it."

"Oh, so maybe he did have a motive."

"Maybe, but he also says he'd never even talked to his sister about it. It just irked him that she had control of half. We also can't find anyone that's ever seen him get violent. Previous arrests were all for public intoxication. He gets rowdy but usually turns into a blubbering mess rather than a crazy person that would kill." He takes a deep breath and looks around. "It just doesn't make sense to me." Taking a step back, he shrugs. "But nobody cares if it makes sense to me, do they?"

I nod and walk past him to get into my car. Eden joins me, madder than ever.

I try to calm her down. "Honey, Aiden's just trying to get Sarah to cooperate. I'm sure he doesn't mean anything by it."

"I know." Her head is hanging, and she sniffles. The tattoo flower on her cheek is flushed a bright pink, and with her head bent, I can see a string of words inked across her shoulder. I keep trying to get a closer look to see what they say, but her shirt strap is always in the way. I'd just ask her, but I'm not sure if that's polite in tattoo manners.

As we turn onto the highway to head toward The Circle, she suddenly laughs. She's resting her head on the headrest and taking long, slow breaths between bits of shallow laughter.

"What's so funny?"

After a deep pull in and release of air, she explains. "I absolutely detest jealousy. Ask any of my friends and they'll tell you I've ranted about it to them. A lot. I can't stand to see a girl act like she owns some guy." Pulling down the visor she wipes her face and talks to the mirror. "'Drop him!' I'd say. If you can't trust him, you don't want him."

Smiling, I lean to catch her eye in the mirror. "But…"

"But it's not that easy, is it?"

"No," I answer. "It isn't. Aiden is a good guy. Does he give you reason to be jealous often?"

She shakes her head. "Never." After a pause she says, "Maybe he was just trying to get her to talk."

We pull into the big parking lot where an old store has been broken into several ventures through the years. The Circle restaurant is at the end, so we park there and get out of the car.

Walking across the asphalt, she shudders and crosses her arms across her chest. "I guess I solved one mystery."

"Yeah? What mystery is that?"

She looks at me and grimaces. "I love him."

I laugh, lay my arm across her shoulders, and give her a squeeze. "Don't worry. It gets so much easier from here."

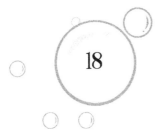

18

"Amber, can I talk to you?" Aiden asks when he reaches our table. "Alone!" he adds as the rest of the Bryant clan turns toward him.

He's still in his uniform, and Sarah is standing behind him. As Amber gets up from her seat, he turns to Sarah and points her toward the ordering line. He turns back toward us to see his mother also getting out of her chair. "No, Momma. Just Amber."

Annie flits a hand in his direction, steps back to the table, and grabs her big cup. "I was just getting a refill. Anyone else need a refill?" She doesn't wait for anyone to hand her their cups as she struts away from us.

The Circle is big and wide open with counter service. Eden was right when she said that they have a wide variety of food. I ordered a delicious Thai chicken salad. Our long table is really several tables put together along the far wall. Annie has six children, and now that Aiden has arrived, four of the six are here: Abigale, Adam, Amber, and Aiden.

I'm seated beside Annie's oldest, Abigale the lawyer. I got to know her last month when she tried to help clear Craig of suspicion. I say "tried" because Craig never felt he needed any help. As usual. Abigale's surfer husband is seated across from her, and on either side of him are Amber's children, Leah and Markie. He seems to fit right in with the kids. Adam, the next oldest, a manager at the marina whom I've met before, is at the table on the end with his wife and two kids; they seem as if they aren't actually part of the crowd.

The two missing are Allie and Annabelle. No one apparently misses Allie, as she's sour and complains about everything. I've only met her once, and I sure don't miss her. Annabelle is the youngest and the only Bryant child I haven't met. She lives at home with her mother and Aiden, and that's really all I know about her.

Aiden strides off toward the front door,

away from his mother and her alleged refill at the drink station. He holds the door open and waits for his sister to saunter through. Amber is heavyset like her mother, and she saunters really well. She is trying to look bored, but it's not working.

Adam leans toward Abigale and says under his breath, "You've warned her. I've warned her. You can't play fast and loose with the law. It was bound to catch up with her eventually." Though he was speaking quietly, it's obvious he wanted us all to hear.

Abigale nods and sighs, but her husband, whom I only know as the "surfer guy," speaks up. "You sure took advantage of her playing fast and loose with the law when you needed a cheap place to live, didn't you?" He laughs and tosses his long hair back. "How long was it you two were separated? Six months? Seven? You know that was the only place on this island you could afford without moving back home with your mother, right?"

I'm beginning to see that Annie's dislike of Abigale's husband might be due to more than just the fact that he likes to surf all day.

"Denny! Shut up," Abigale hisses. "Momma doesn't know." Her eyes are darting around the restaurant looking for her mother.

Okay, I think, as I spear a slice of cucumber on my fork, his name is Denny.

"Puh-lease," he says with another laugh. "Your mother knows everything that goes on here. Give her a little credit." He leans forward on his elbows. "Everybody is so worried about how this poor girl's death will affect them that no one is even mourning her." In a falsetto, singsong voice, he says, "Amber's rentals, the shrimp festival, and what about the turtles? Oh my!"

Adam's wife suddenly stands up. "That's it. We're leaving. Kids, go say goodbye to Grandma."

As they gather their things, Abigale glares at her husband, but Denny just shakes his head in disgust and looks out the front windows. Suddenly she blurts out, "You knew her. Leslie Callahan. You were friends!"

Denny takes a breath and scoots his chair out. "Yeah. From the beach. She was a really talented artist. I know all the people, if you even think of them as people, that live up in your sister's rooms in The Settlement." He stands, then looks down with his hands on his hips and his hair hiding his face. "It was all coming out, you know." He looks up at his wife and then his brother-in-law. "I tried to warn Amber too. It all had to come out sometime." As he turns away, he sees Sarah heading in our direction with her tray. "Hey there," he whispers, and he meets her with a hug to the side.

Adam's wife and kids are already halfway to the front door, but he's still standing over Abigale. Now he looks down at her. "Your husband is a real winner. I'm so glad I brought my family tonight." He pushes through the chairs and leaves.

Oh, siblings and spouses. So many buttons to push, so little time.

Denny brings Sarah over to the table. "Leah, can my friend have your chair? You can sit beside your aunt Abigale, okay?"

"Okay," the girl answers. "Are we still going to Dairy Queen? Did Momma leave?"

Abigale pulls the chair Adam left closer to her and pats it for her niece. "No, she's just talking to Uncle Aiden. And of course Grandma will take you to get ice cream."

Denny takes his seat with a roll of his eyes and a grin at me. I grin back but watch as Annie gives him the evil eye on her approach. "So, Adam and his crew had to leave. Why am I not surprised?" she mumbles in Denny's direction.

Then she brightens up and raises her voice. "Sorry, I got distracted talking to people. You know how I am!" Annie's eyes are lively as she bustles back to her seat beside me. "Hello, Sarah. I haven't seen you in a long time."

I chuckle to myself. Of course she knows Sarah. It's completely laughable that her kids think she wouldn't know about Adam being separated from his wife and living up at The Settlement. I have to give that one to Denny. It does seem a person's own kids are often the least knowledgeable about their parents as people.

Sarah looks up from her bowl of soup. "Yes, ma'am. It has been a while."

There's a pause, but then Abigale the lawyer can't stand it. "Momma, how do you know Sarah?"

"Sarah helped at Vacation Bible School last year, didn't you? She helped in the art tent." Annie sits straighter, her head lifted. "Here they come," she says loudly.

I look up to see Amber and Aiden walking toward us. Amber looks worried. Aiden looks exhausted. She takes her seat at the end of the table near her mother. Aiden stops and rests his hands on the back of Markie's chair as he says, "Sorry, Momma, but I've got to go back to the station. Some stuff has come up." He doesn't look anywhere but at his mother. Eden has been quiet through everything, sitting between me and Annie. She starts to stand u but he waves a hand at her. "Don't get up. Miss Jewel, can you and Eden give Sarah a ride? I'll come by the house when I'm done."

"But you didn't eat anything!" Annie exclaims. "Let me get you a sandwich to take with you."

"No, Momma. Thanks, but I'm not hungry." His eyes slide to Amber, and his voice gets husky. "Kinda lost my appetite."

He turns around and walks off, leaving us all to share glances and questioning looks—all except for Amber, who is staring at her plate. Then she says, "Leah and Markie, y'all go play some of those games." She pulls her purse off the back of her chair. "Here's some quarters." The kids don't have to be told twice. They hurry to collect their quarters and then jog back toward the drink station, where there's a little alcove with a couple of arcade games.

Abigale leans one elbow on the table so that she can see around me, Eden, and her mother to stare at her sister. "What? The Settlement? You're in trouble, aren't you? Adam and I tried to warn you, but you've never been able to turn down a dollar."

Denny shakes his head at his wife. "Let her talk."

Eden turns to me. "Can you let me out? Sarah and I will go sit over there. This feels like family business."

Amber looks up and smiles her gratitude at Eden, and Abigale and I get up to let her out. Sarah picks up her tray and follows Eden. I'm the only one that knows how upset Eden was with Sarah flirting with Aiden earlier, so I'm the only one who knows how hard this must be for her. I turn to the table and say, "Why don't I join them? Let you four talk."

Amber looks up. "No. Please stay. I think I'm going to need your help."

"Okay, but I don't know anything about housing laws." I add a chuckle, hoping to lighten the mood as I slide back into my seat.

Amber's face settles downward, as if it's tired of staying in a more uplifted position. She looks so sad. It takes effort for her to open her mouth, but finally she does. "It's not about The Settlement. Well, not exactly."

Annie doesn't look up at her, and I realize that whatever her daughter is getting ready to say, she already knows.

Amber addresses her anyway. "Momma, Mark and I, well, we're—uh. We…"

Annie finally looks up. "I know. You and Mark are getting back together. That's fine. Now you can quit all the sneaking around."

Denny grins and slaps the table. "That's all? You look like someone died. Let's go get some ice cream." As he starts to push his chair back, Abigale stretches out her hand and lays it on his arm to stop him. I don't think she thinks her sister is through.

Amber wrinkles her nose. "That's not exactly all. We're not getting back together, but sometimes we get together. You know…"

"Mercy sakes, Amber Marie!" Annie exclaims. "I don't want to hear about your carrying on! For once I'm with Denny; let's go get ice cream. Move so I can get out of here."

Abigale holds out her other arm to stop her mother. "Wait. What else is it, Amber? Quit being so dramatic!"

"Oh, you think I'm being dramatic?" Amber squares off like only a sister can, her chin pushed out and eyes flaring. "How about this? How about I was with Mark Sunday night on the beach? How about I'm his alibi? You like that, Miss Lawyer of the Year?"

Annie is stunned, her blue eyes wider than I've ever seen them. Denny looks confused, and then I look at Abigale. Her eyes are squinted, and her lips are pressed tight.

Quietly she says, "You were on the beach Sunday night?"

"Yes, but Mark was protecting me by not telling everyone. It just seems so, uh, *unseemly* to be rolling around in the sand like a couple of teenagers." Her face still bowed, she adds, "Just so embarrassing."

"Oh, Amber," her sister laments. "Don't you see? You didn't clear Mark; you placed yourself at the murder scene of a girl paying you under the table for an illegal place to live. Which, as I've said before, jeopardizes your career and probably everything you own once the IRS gets involved." She sighs, and her shoulders sink. "Honey, your motive for wanting Leslie Callahan out of the way is much stronger than anything they have on Mark."

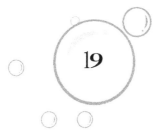

19

This reminds me of being in college when my roommate wanted to be alone with her boyfriend. I'm climbing the stairs, leaving Eden and Aiden cuddled on the settee. Sarah is climbing the stairs in front of me. She's apparently been read the riot act about flirting with Aiden as she was on her best behavior tonight once he arrived. She steps into the first room at the top of the stairs, and I follow her, just to the doorway.

"You have everything you need? Air mattress comfortable enough?"

She drops to her knees beside her stuffed book bag and unzips it. "Yes, ma'am. Thank you for letting me stay here. I only have one more final, and then I'm done."

"Are you taking classes this summer?"

She shrugs without looking up and keeps digging in her bag, pulling out a phone cord and clothes.

"Well," I say and push away from the doorframe.

"My folks want me to come live with them in Texas."

"You can always go to school there."

"Yeah. That was what they wanted from the beginning, but I thought I was good on my own. Look how that turned out." She surveys her sleeping arrangement, which she told me earlier is pretty much how it was with Leslie up in The Settlement. "I don't think I got as much from my classes as I should've." Looking up at me, she tries a half smile. "Besides, most of my friends have moved on. And, well, Leslie…" She drops her head and concentrates on her book bag, pulling out a small sketchpad and laying it on the bed.

"Oh. Did you find Leslie's sketchpads in your things this morning?" I'd forgotten that that's what they were looking for in her car.

"Just old ones. No pictures that could've been her dad. The one she was using Sunday is missing, I guess."

"Missing? That's odd. Do they think the person who killed her took it?"

She moves off her knees to sit cross-legged on the floor. "I don't know. I've got to get some sleep. Can you close the door?" Again she looks up with a smile, apologizing with her sad eyes.

"Sure. Sleep tight, and just for the record, I think going to your parents is a great idea. If I can help, just let me know."

"Okay. Maybe a ride to the airport after the funeral? But I'll let you know. Good night."

She's already turning away from me, so I don't ask if she knows any details about the funeral. I pull the door shut and walk down the hallway, all the way to the end, where my bedroom is on the front of the house. Closing my door, I find my way to the bedside table and turn on the lamp. I take a pad of paper out of the drawer, unpile a stack of clothes from the chair beside the bay window, and sit down.

Annie put out a text earlier calling for a meeting in the morning. According to her, we need to put our detective hats back on. Lucy tried to beg off, saying she was up to her neck in turtle business. Annie, in all caps and with multiple exclamation points, explained that Amber had moved up to number one suspect and then expressed a not-very-nice opinion on turtles.

Needless to say, Lucy will be there, as will Cherry, Tamela, and myself.

Before I forget again I jot down, "Sketchpad?" Beside it I write, "How did she die?" Aiden may be filling Eden in on some of the details downstairs. He couldn't really talk in front of Sarah, and besides, he had some making up to do with his girlfriend. I realize I don't even know what Leslie looked like. Going to Google, I find a list of news articles from nearby Jacksonville. "Body Found in Turtle Nest" is one headline. Another screams, "Murder on the Beach," then follows up with the still-lurid: "Horror on Sophia Island." I can see why the chamber of commerce people are concerned.

Clicking on the top story, I find two pictures of Leslie Callahan. One looks like a yearbook photo. The other is probably from social media as she's pulling a duck face, puckering her lips and looking up through her eyelashes. She has long, brown hair, brown eyes. Studying the picture from social media, I see that she definitely looks older in it. Tired. Maybe it's a recent picture. I can see Eustis in her, the long face and nose. Her eyes are not the light gray of her mother and brother. They're dark and a solid brown.

I move away from the pictures because they're just too sad, so I read the article. It doesn't take long to see why she looked so much older in the more recent picture. She dropped out of school her senior year and moved to the beach. That would've been at least six years ago. Waitressing, living in a room in an old house, and hanging out on the beach will age you fast.

I try to imagine any of my four leaving school and home at the drop of a hat. She wasn't that far from home, so why didn't Eustis come get her? Maybe she did. Can you make a kid come home if they're eighteen? Eustis seems like she was pretty removed from her daughter. Did she even want her to come home?

All of these questions float around inside my brain, but I don't write them down. Then one question jumps out. Her father. Her real father. How did she find him? I hurriedly write that down, then add, "Or did he find her?" Below that, I scrawl, "GED? He paid for college—financial records?"

My pen is suddenly going faster than my brain, and I fill up two sheets of questions and comments. I realize I've been thinking about all this but not in any orderly way.

Finally I lay the notepad to one side and stand up to stretch. I intentionally didn't listen out for Eden when she came up the stairs a while ago, and I intentionally didn't hear her whispering to someone before her door closed. I brush my teeth and change into my pajamas, and then, sitting on the edge of my bed, I set an alarm on my phone. I turn out the lamp and lie in bed scrolling through my phone. When was the last time I talked to Craig? It's a couple swipes down my recent calls list before I see his name. The same goes for my list of text messages. Maybe I should send him a quick text; it's definitely too late to call. I procrastinate, though, playing around on Google, and Leslie Callahan's picture comes up again. Her graduation picture. Those same dark eyes, hair falling straight down from a center part. She's wearing a light-blue shirt with a collar.

With a sigh I realize I almost care more about her than I do my husband.

I lay my phone down and go to sleep.

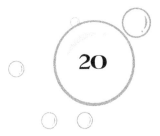

20

"What do you mean you've never had biscuits and gravy?" Annie asks, her eyes squeezed in disbelief, her nose wrinkled in disgust, and her perfectly lipsticked, coral-hued mouth distorted in horror. Cherry is grinning and Tamela adds a cute sigh to her sad, sad look.

Lucy is tapping on her phone and misses the whole thing.

"Like gravy from roast beef? On a biscuit?" I ask. "I mean, I've heard of them; they just never have sounded appetizing."

Annie lays her plastic menu on the table and rests her folded arms on it. "Sausage gravy. They even put pieces of sausage in their gravy here. Y'all ready to order?" She looks around for our waitress.

I hide behind my menu. Gravy made with sausage grease? My stomach is not ready for that. I tried the shrimp and grits everyone here raves about, forced by you-know-who, and they were okay. But now I'm supposed to get excited about pieces of sausage? Chunks of link sausage? In greasy gravy? I do like biscuits, so why would I ruin them?

I blink back to reality to find that everyone else has ordered, but Annie is still talking to the waitress and I think I'm involved. Everyone is looking at me, including the waitress.

"So, besides the biscuits and gravy your friend ordered for you, what can I get you?" she asks.

"I did want the pancakes, but that sounds a bit carb-heavy with a biscuit and gravy, doesn't it?" I say, heavy on the smirk.

Annie smiles and says, "You'll thank me later. I'm going to the bathroom."

"I'll take the Sunny Special. Eggs scrambled, bacon, and rye toast," I say as I hand the waitress my menu. She whirls away to deal with one of her other tables.

We are only a couple of blocks from my house in the historic district. Sunny Side Up is in a one-story house with a small outdoor area that looks to have been the driveway many years ago. There's covered seating where a carport would have been, and the restrooms are in a shed at the back of the carport. Then there's more outdoor seating around the back. The inside looks tiny, but since they're only open in the mornings I imagine most everyone likes sitting outside. I've not been here before. I think I've walked and driven by the restaurant before, but I never noticed it before Annie invited me this morning. It seems a lot of the places here are like that. You have to know where and what they are before you ever think of visiting them. Advertising isn't a priority unless a place is on the main roads. Those places try to draw you in with menus out front and nice signage, but places like Sunny Side Up? Not so much.

Cherry echoes just what I was thinking. "Never knew this place was here. Looks like it's been around a long time."

"Yep," Tamela says. "They've gone through some ups and downs, but right now they're doing well, I've heard."

Lucy yelps and holds her phone to her chest. As we all try to figure out what's going on, she looks out front toward the road. "Oh, my lord in heaven. They *cannot* be coming here!"

Annie rushes back to our table, grabs her seat, and whispers as she drops into it, "Lucy, d'you see who just walked in?" She's frowning, but her eyes sparkle with mischief.

My back is to the entrance, so Tamela leans over to whisper, "Awful Sheila Hornsby, that woman who was at the turtle nest, and she's got Benjamin Perkins with her."

Of course I remember the turtle lady, and the man's name sounds familiar. Then they walk past us heading for the tables around back, and I realize it's the young man with the pregnant wife who lives near Lucy. He was also at the town meeting the night we found out that the fake nest was a grave.

"Benjamin! Sheila! Good morning!" Lucy bounces up like she's leading cheers at a football game, causing them to turn around.

Sheila looks as unhappy and unkempt as she did on the beach that day. She squints at Lucy, and I know she's skeptical. Heck, I'm skeptical. It doesn't take long to work out that whole "bless your heart" thing isn't as well-intentioned as it might sound.

Sheila shoves a hand out like she wants to shake Lucy's, but it's really to ward off a big hug. Benjamin, however, in his starched white shirt and tie, accepts his hug with a smile and an extra squeeze. This young man's planning a career in Southern politics, so he knows his role.

Introducing all of us, Lucy smiles and honestly appears to flirt with Benjamin, who meets each of our eyes and shakes our hands. Sheila scowls at everyone. I'm the last to be introduced.

"Aw, the famous Mrs. Mantelle." Benjamin presses my hand in his, then slowly disengages by sliding out of my grip, letting my fingertips rest in his. He winks and says, "What I wouldn't give for a look at that house of yours. It's simply fascinating. I remember when the old Mrs. Mantelle would sit and look out that upstairs window. It felt positively ghostly. I was sorry to hear she had to be institutionalized." He tightens his grip on my fingers. "Please tell me I can come by for a tour."

I blush. I know I do not only because of the heat I feel on my face, but because of the grins of my breakfast companions. I swallow, then choke out, "Yes, you should come see it. Oh! And congratulations on the baby. When is your wife due?"

"July. Thank you." He pulls back. "Well, ladies, we'll leave you to your morning. Wonderful to meet all of you."

Lucy grabs his arm and sways toward him

as her accent gets thicker. "Y'all look like you've got just a passel of work to do what with all them folders. Benjamin, honey, it's just a shame you have to carry around that briefcase on such a beautiful day! We'd ask y'all to join us, but we've already ordered and our manners just wouldn't allow us to eat in front of you." With a cute frown, she sits back down, then gives them a cute finger wave as she says, "Enjoy your breakfast!"

Annie stares them down all the way to their table. "Sheila might've run a comb through that hair before she came out in public." She tips her head and clicks her tongue. "But that Perkins boy sure does make up for her lack of sprucing up. If I looked that good in a dress shirt, I'd wear them all the time too."

Lucy gives her a death stare. "He's the enemy as much as Sheila is. Maybe more. He's finding every little loophole in our charter and making us look like country fools. He's setting up a network of all the turtle groups in the state. Just imagine how that'll help him win a statewide election." She lifts, then looks into her empty coffee cup. "Where is my refill?" She raises her mug higher and smiles over my head. "If she wants my usual tip, she better get over here. I'm not in the mood to be nice for much longer."

Looking away from that oncoming disaster, I turn my attention across the table. "So, Annie, how's Amber?" I add in a whisper, "Have you heard anything from the police? Is Aiden still allowed to work on the case?"

She shakes her silver curls and takes a deep breath. "It's all so much better than last night. First thing this morning Abigale went down to the station and found out Amber is *not* a suspect." But then she winces. "This is gruesome, y'all, but that poor girl was strangled. The suspect most likely couldn't be a woman from how deep the bruising is." Tamela and I join her in wincing. Lucy is still a million miles away, and Cherry nods like the professional nurse she is.

"So are they even more settled on Mark?" Tamela asks. She avoids my look. She is so determined he's innocent, though I don't understand why.

Annie sighs and waits for the waitress, who arrives in a flurry to refill all our cups.

"Y'all's food will be right out," she says as she hurries away again. I'd hurry, too, if I was getting that stare from Lucy.

Lucy takes a sip of her fresh coffee. "Okay, ladies, I'm sorry for daydreaming. I'm putting all the turtle stuff on the back burner and paying attention now. I heard that Amber is in the clear, and please do not repeat that awful reason why. Now, Mark?"

"You're amazing," Annie says. "The way you multitask. I'm doing good if I'm getting one thing done at a time!" She laughs. "Anyway. Mark may also be in the clear now since Amber is admitting they were together. They left the beach together and went to get gas. She has her receipt, but they are hoping a camera at the gas station also caught Mark in the car."

"Gas stations on Sophia have cameras?" I ask.

Cherry smirks. "I was just thinking the same thing!"

Lucy's mouth drops in insult. "What? I'll have you know this is not just some backwater beach town. Of course we have cameras."

Tamela sniffs. "Of course we have cameras. They're installed on every traffic light on the main road. Now, are they connected to anything and actually operational?" She shrugs and cuts her eyes at Lucy.

Lucy cocks her head. "We have cameras, and that's what matters. All that other stuff will come eventually. This looks like our food."

As our garden table fills with dishes and hot food, then is slowly emptied of dirty dishes and leftovers, we talk about the questions we have concerning the murder of Leslie Callahan. Then we divvy up the questions to those most able to find the answers.

Our bills paid, we walk out front. Lucy groans. "We should all walk home like Jewel after that big breakfast."

"You're welcome to join me," I say. "I'm cleaning the insides of all the windows today. You should come see the difference Eden's made."

Cherry stretches her arms above her head as we stand in the shade beside the cars. "Yes, I really want to see it with the curtains and carpet gone. How about pizza and wine at your house tonight? I have to work the next two nights." She lowers her arms. "Plus that'll force us to do some detecting today and get at least a few answers. Or maybe even come up with more questions. If Mark didn't kill his sister, who did? At the very least, maybe after we talk tonight we can push the police to do some more investigating."

Annie puts her hands on her wide hips and cocks her head. "I have more faith in us than that. We're good at this detective stuff."

Lucy is putting something in her phone.

"Okay, my calendar is empty, so I can do tonight at Jewel's. I'll bring wine."

"Sure, it's okay with me," I say. "I'll order the pizza."

"Salad," Tamela says, holding her hand up.

"Yum, that means I get to bring dessert," Cherry says. "Maybe Jo will make something; she loves baking. Her being back home sure hasn't helped Martin with his diet, but we might as well benefit from it too."

"Is six okay?" I say as I walk toward the street and they head for their cars.

They all nod, and then Annie hollers as she opens her car door. "I was going to get out of here and not say anything, but I just can't do it. Miss Jewel, don't think I didn't see your biscuits and gravy plate was licked plumb clean!" She explodes with a big laugh followed by a smug look.

With a tip of my head to her, I turn to walk down the sandy street bordered by big trees. Sunny Side Up is such a neat place and so close to our house. It'll be perfect to bring the kids to when they're all here for Memorial Day.

And I'm ordering biscuits and gravy for us all, whether they like it or not!

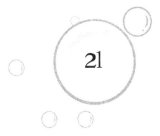

21

Mornings on Sophia Island are quickly becoming my favorite time of day. Walking along the street to our house from the restaurant, it's quiet. The school buses have run; people are at their jobs. The streets belong to the lawn maintenance folks and a few dog walkers. The shade is plentiful, with the sun still rising to its noontime high out at the beach. On the rare morning the smell of the paper mill is pungent or the noise invasive, but even those things are becoming familiar and not off-putting.

While many aspects of this move have failed miserably to match my expectations, one area is trying to make up for the rest. I've always wanted a hometown, a place to settle. My father didn't like owning a house, so we always rented when I was growing up. He traveled a lot with his job and my mom was obsessed with first law school, then her career, so she didn't want owning a house to take up any of her time. When our rental house would become too expensive or be put up for sale, we'd simply move. My brother chose a career in the military, and I chose a husband whose job meant frequent moves. Moving was part of our DNA. Craig and I would move to be near his next project, with me naively hoping our proximity would mean he'd be home more often.

I pull my phone out of my pocket. It seems a shame to mess with this good mood I'm in, but I promised myself I'd call Craig this morning on my walk home.

"Hi," he says, picking up on the first ring. "What's up?"

"I haven't heard from you in a while, so I thought I'd call and check in on you. How are things going?"

"Good. How about you?" Before I can answer he asks, "Can you hold on a minute?"

He's talking to some other people, but I can only hear voices, not words. "Okay, I'm back. Just needed to get those guys started. So, what do you need?"

"Nothing. Just wanted to say hello." I stop and sit on an old concrete wall along the sidewalk in front of a house. My heart is beating quickly and I can't seem to catch my breath, but I try to be nonchalant. "The kids are all planning on being here for Memorial Day weekend. You knew that, right?"

"I think so. Erin told me. She likes to keep everyone informed," he says with a chuckle.

Oh, it feels nice to hear him laugh. I chuckle, too, and my shoulders relax a bit. "She sure does. So you'll be here, right?"

"Of course. Wouldn't miss it." He sounds light, happy.

"Good. Will you be able to come home before then? That's over a month away."

"Home? You mean there?"

I clear my throat. "Yeah, here. Where else?"

"No need to get snarky," he says. "You know how I feel about that place. I'm in the middle of all this, and there's no need for me to drive all that way just to be miserable."

"I sure wouldn't want you to be miserable." I jump up from my seat and stride down the sidewalk.

He snaps back at me. "I don't see you rushing down here to see me, and you have all the time in the world."

"Oh! I'm invited down there?" I'm in full-on snark mode now.

"Of course. Why wouldn't you be? You could shop and see the sights around Fort Lauderdale. The beach is nice here."

I pause before crossing the street. "Wait, do you really want me to come down there?" My heartbeat has slowed down, but it feels heavy as I wait for him to answer. He's talking again to someone else, and then he comes back to the phone.

"Sorry. It's busy here, but sure. Come down sometime if you want. As long as you don't plan on me entertaining you. It's not a vacation for me. Someone has to work."

Neither of us speaks for a moment, and then I say, "You're busy, but we really need to talk. Can we talk tonight? What time would be good for you?"

"Tonight?" I hear him shuffling papers. "Sure, I'll try, but Jewel…"

"What?" I ask after pulling in a calming breath when he doesn't finish his thought.

"I'm just kind of done with all this back-and-forth confusion, aren't you? None of this even seems real to me anymore. It's exhausting."

I look around. All of this was so unfamiliar only a few months—no, *weeks* ago.

Our three-story house looms across the street with the black iron fence around it and all those windows staring at me. By day's end I will have cleaned each one of them. The palm trees and that tall, full bush covered with pink flowers, the sand everywhere, is all so new, but all of it is so real. So mine.

After a swallow I choke out, "We need to talk. I'll call you tonight—oh, no, I can't tonight. Tomorrow night." I bite my tongue to keep me from saying anything more.

"Sounds good. I'll be around." He hangs up without saying goodbye.

No problem. It feels like we said our goodbyes already.

"Anyone home?" comes Officer Greyson's inquiry from below.

"Yes! Me. I'm coming!" I shout from the third floor. It's a small area at the top of a narrow set of steps, only one room, but with several windows. It's still stuffed with furniture and junk, but Eden and I decided to ignore everything up there and concentrate on the floors we use. However, I said I was washing all the windows, and that meant even the ones on the third floor. I'm proud of the progress I've made, and it's not even one o'clock yet.

Brushing dust off the old shorts I wear for painting and a ratty T-shirt I stole from one of our boys, I step into the second-floor hall and dash to the top of the staircase. "Here I am!" I shout, looking down as I descend. I'm unsure why he's stopped by, but I assume it's about his investigation. Good, since I'll need something to tell my friends later over pizza.

Officer Greyson walks toward the stairs. "The front door was ajar. That's not safe when you're here alone." He frowns and shakes his head. "Actually it's not safe when you're not here alone."

"Eden ran over here on her lunch break. She must not have closed it when she left." In the living room, I flop onto my chaise and wave a hand at him. "Have a seat. What can I do for you?"

Instead of sitting he wanders around the room. "Y'all have really gotten a lot done. This looks more like a home than a junk shop now."

"I agree. Eden is a wonder."

He finally takes a seat across from me. "So you know Amber is trying to give her ex an alibi?"

"You make it sound like she's lying," I say.

"Besides, if the gas station caught a picture of them they'd both be in the clear."

"That gas station doesn't have cameras." He looks at me like I'm crazy, but I refrain from saying that's what I thought. He frowns again. "That's the same argument Amber's trying to make. Her sister is going door to door looking for one of the residents that might have a security camera that got a picture of them."

"But Amber is in the clear, right? It was definitely a man?"

"Or a woman with really large hands, but most probably a man. Mark was released last night. We haven't found anything else to tie him to the crime, but we're still looking."

I clear my throat and look away from him. "Was Leslie hurt in any other way? No one has said."

He pauses, then catches on. "Oh, was she raped or sexually assaulted? No."

"That's a relief to hear." I get up. "I need a glass of water. Can I get you one?"

I hear him stand as he says, "No, I'm good. Thanks." He walks in and stands close to the kitchen table, looking out the window. "I see the trimmers have been busy."

"Oh, that's why it looks so light in here." I hurry to the window. "Look at that. I didn't even hear them from upstairs. Friends of Eden's father."

He raises one eyebrow at me and chuckles. "Um, Ted? Yeah, Ted knows a lot of people."

"What? He's been very helpful."

He smiles and lifts both eyebrows this time. "Ted is often perceived to be helpful." He raises his hands when my mouth drops open to protest. "Ignore me. It's not always good to have grown up here. Hard to give up my biases."

Giving him a smug look, I walk past him to the front door and step outside. It's hard to tell what's been trimmed with all the clippings piled everywhere. "I'm sure they're coming back to clean all this up."

From behind me comes a very sweet, "Oh, absolutely," followed by a chuckle.

Walking back inside, I ask again, "What's next with the investigation?"

Greyson clicks his tongue. "Nothing really. We found out where Leslie was earlier that evening after Sarah left, but it doesn't have a connection to her murder."

"Where was she?"

He turns away from me to look out the front porch windows. "That doesn't really matter. I think we have to realize Leslie was a troubled young woman. She led a hard life, and we know there were some unsavory types on the beach that night. Remember the near-riot down at Peele's Point?"

"Riot? I know there were a lot of college kids, but I don't remember anyone calling it a riot." I move around to face him. He doesn't move but keeps looking out the window.

"Whatever. Her time is accounted for, and she was out on the beach after dark. Wrong place, wrong time."

My jaw drops. "Are you serious? If she lived in one of those beach mansions you can bet no one would be saying, 'Wrong place, wrong time'!"

He stretches his head to the side like his neck muscles are tight. "Don't get the wrong idea, we're still investigating. We've just run out of leads. Leslie was last seen heading down the beach in the dark, toward the group of partying kids." He lifts one hand to the back of his neck and kneads it.

"Last seen? Who was she last seen by?" I ask his back.

After a moment he turns to face me, meet my eyes, and shake his head. "I've been told that's not important." I think he's trying to tell me something, but then he slumps. "Honestly, the source is unimpeachable and verified. I better be leaving. I'm meeting Aiden at three to look into the kids who were on the beach on Sunday night."

He pulls open the front door and steps out, saying, "I'll let you get back to—"

"Her father! The family dinner! That's where she left from, isn't it?" I rush to follow him out onto the porch.

He shrugs. "Let's just say we have good eyewitness accounts of her leaving alone and heading in that direction. It's unorthodox, but I guess I can see why putting all of that out in the open would mean tearing this person's family apart." He steps closer to me and lowers his voice. "He never got to tell his family she was his daughter. Everyone agrees there's no need to make it public knowledge now."

"Now that she's dead? Are you kidding me? No one sees this as a motive?"

"No. No, *they* don't." He stares at me, then walks to the steps and descends them. At the bottom, with a light laugh he adds, "Good luck with the house. Tell Ted I said hello."

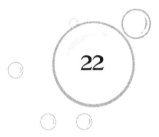

22

"Eustis is missing," Annie announces before I can even say hello.

After Greyson left I quickly finished the last few windows and ran out to get groceries. "Missing?" I say into my phone. "Since when? She was on the news—was that yesterday? Or, no, the day before, right?"

"Nope. Yesterday. Wednesday morning. It does seem like a million years ago, doesn't it?" Annie's sigh points out just how long this week has been already.

Squeezing my phone between my shoulder and ear, I say, "Hey, I'm checking out at Publix. Can I call you right back?"

She perks right up. "Oh! I'm across the

street getting the kids ice cream at Tribiani's. Come join us."

"That's down toward the beach, right? Brightly colored building? I'll be right there." I hit the end button with a quick "sorry" to the lady checking me out. Luckily I don't have anything for the freezer, so I can run over to see Annie for a bit. Gone for me are the winter days up north where even frozen groceries could be left in the car while I continued my errands. Not a bad tradeoff if you ask me.

On Statler Avenue the island feels like a beach town, especially the closer I get to the end where the road drops away to sand and surf. A couple hotels, seafood restaurants, a biker bar, and a surf shop serve as ground zero for the vacationers not staying farther south at one of the luxury resorts. Many people rent vacation homes in this area, both on and across the street from the beach.

Tribiani's is a one-story, concrete-block, brightly painted building that I've passed many times but never stopped in. They have a little play area, and I quickly spot Leah and Markie eyeing the play equipment while they finish their cones. "Hey, guys!" I say.

Leah points behind her. "Grandma's over there."

"What kind of ice cream did you get?"

With a practiced lick, she says, "Strawberry. Markie got chocolate." She wearily shakes her head. "He always makes such a mess."

Markie grins and nods, chocolate covering half his face and running down both hands.

"Do you need a napkin?" I ask.

Leah holds up a stack with her empty hand. "He doesn't want one. Grandma said she was tired of fighting with him." Her older-sister burden calls for a sigh and another shake of her tiny head. "He's a handful for sure."

With a laugh, I walk over to where Annie is seated at a picnic table. "She sounds just like you."

"Good thing I'm such a good influence, isn't it?" She winks as she wads up her napkin and puts it in her empty ice cream cup. "Don't you want a scoop?"

"I can't stay long." I sit across from her. "So what's this about Eustis missing?"

Her eyes flick to the children. "Mark got released last night like we hoped, and when he got home she wasn't there. He waited until this morning to call around to some friends and see if she was staying with any of them. He wasn't too worried at first, but he got worried pretty quick when no one knew where she might be."

"Did he call the police?"

"Not yet. Her purse is gone, but the only phone she has is an old flip phone and that's at the house. He says she didn't carry it around unless she thought she'd need it. But no clothes are gone that he can tell." She waves at Markie, who waves back at us from the top of the colorful slide. "The dogs were outside and hungry, and everyone agrees there's no way she'd leave her dogs hungry. Nothing is messed up, though. It looks like she just left yesterday morning and didn't go home."

"No one's seen her since the press conference?"

Annie shakes her head, and sadness settles across her face. "I don't know what to think. There's Leslie's funeral to plan. Can't do that without her mother."

"Oh, I guess not. Can I help with anything?"

She plants her hands on the table and pushes up from the bench. "Just have the wine chilled and the pizza hot tonight. I need a girls' night."

I watch as she moves to the fence and informs her grandkids that it's time to go home. They bombard her with questions about where they're going next and if their momma is going to be home. Did they find Mamaw? Does Daddy have to go back to jail? Annie handles every question while urging them to "come on." Finally all three are headed back to the table, so I stand up.

"It was good to see you guys again," I tell the kids. Then I smile at Annie. "And I'll see you in just a bit. Cold wine. Hot pizza."

"Can we have pizza?" Markie asks.

"We'll see," his grandmother says, steering him to her car. "First it's going to take a half pack of wipes to get you clean before I let you in my car. See you later, Jewel."

I decide to drive A1A along the beach on my way home. There are enough cars to keep it from feeling deserted, but I know this stretch is nothing like it will be in a few weeks. I know this because everyone keeps warning me that the hordes and the heat are coming. Parking spots downtown, easy seating in restaurants, and short lines at the grocery will be mere fantasy soon. Apparently the short time we've lived here is one of two sweet spots for locals in the yearly calendar: January until April, with the exception of spring break, and then a few weeks in the fall. They aren't as exact on that second stretch of time because the weather is less predictable then. I think that's their nice, delusional way of saying "hurricane season," but I am definitely not thinking about that. It's tornado time back in the Midwest, and I'm enjoying missing that.

At the main beach I cross the island back to the riverfront and downtown. Passing Fort Clinch State Park, I remember Sarah saying she and Leslie had been drawing there Sunday afternoon. Were they drawing the fort? Nature still-lifes? My assignment from this morning was to talk to Sarah some more, to see if she remembers anything else about that Sunday. I lured her and Eden home with the promise of Publix sub sandwiches, which I must admit are fantastic, so they should be at the house waiting on me, hopefully with lots of new information. After speaking with Officer Greyson, I had called and asked Eden if she could find out from Aiden who Leslie's father is.

I pull into the driveway, and as I weave around yard debris, I think of another thing to ask Eden: When's her father's friend coming to clean all this up?

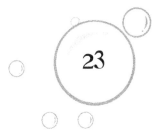

23

"It's the bread. Not too crunchy, but not too soft," Sarah says as she examines the half of the sandwich in her hand. "I sure will miss these in Texas." She stops with the sandwich almost to her mouth. "Wait, or are there Publixes in Texas? I know they're in some other Southern states."

We're sitting on the porch, and while the girls eat I'm looking through Sarah's sketchpad, the one she was using on Sunday. Most of her sketches are of the ocean and the beach, but there are a few of the local grasses and flowers. She explained that she's in a class on drawing nature, so that's been her recent focus.

Eden leans back in her chair. The porch is

still home to the sturdy chairs we don't want in the house, and this one looks like it's from an old dining room set. Mismatched seating is better than no seating. She's wearing a loose linen dress that skims her thin body. It has no shape, but with her short, dark red hair, colorful tattoos, and big eyes, it's striking on her. She's barefoot and looks like she's doing some sort of photo shoot, lounging back in the big, antique dining chair, one bare leg slung over the wooden arm. "Aiden says he has no idea who Leslie's father is. Only a couple of people know and it's gone no further, so we figure it's some big shot. A real big shot, not just someone who thinks of themselves as a big shot. You know."

"Sarah, would it be like Leslie to party with the college kids that were on the beach Sunday night?" I stop flipping pages to watch her reaction.

She wrinkles her nose. "No. She hung out at the bar at the end of Statler. Not the biker bar, but the one upstairs at Dunes, or else she liked the upstairs one at The Crab Pot at the marina." With a grin she adds, "She always said, 'If you know the area bartenders, why would you drink in the sand?'"

Eden laughs. "I never thought about it that way."

Sarah nods as she takes another bite of her sandwich but still manages to say, "Only problem with knowing the bartenders is they know I'm not old enough to drink."

"But you went out drinking after work on Sunday, right?" I remember her saying that because at the time I had wondered how old she was. "Where did you go?"

Her eyes jump over to Eden's but only settle there for a moment while she chews. "Where else? Peele's Point. It was a little rowdy, but there are always coolers of beer and whatnot."

"Why didn't you say that earlier?" Ugh, it's like talking to a cat. "Did you see Leslie there?"

Eden sits up and Sarah swallows. Both look at me like I just magically appeared in front of them. Eden asks, "Is someone saying Leslie was with the kids on the beach?" She leans back again. "That would never happen."

Sarah nods. "Leslie hated those groups. Hated the whole college-kid vibe with a passion." She pauses a minute and admits, "I never told her when I was down there because she'd rip me up one side and down the other."

Eden nods in agreement. "She's right.

In high school we'd all watch out for when there'd be a big bunch of college kids at the point, and we'd try to sneak in once they got drunk and steal beer. Leslie was younger than us, but she was out there a lot. Later, though, she became like an old lady about it. There's no way she was headed to that group."

Sarah frowns. "Who says she went down there? Besides, she was found at the other end of the beach. Nowhere near Peele's."

"That's right." I look back down at the sketchpad and turn pages. They're right; that story doesn't make any sense. As I reach the end of Sarah's drawings, I flip through the empty pages and see some more drawings near the end. As I open to them, Sarah leans toward me.

"What are those?" She pulls the pad toward her and studies the drawings then slowly says, "Oh yeah. Leslie didn't have her sketchpad on Sunday, so she used the back pages of mine. How did I forget that?"

Eden's eyes fly to mine. It looks like we're both thinking, "Yeah, how exactly *did* you forget that?" but a little hiccup from Sarah draws our attention back to her and the missing drawings.

Instead of waves and flowers, these few pages are filled with birds and people. Eden comes over to stand behind us and look. She rubs her bare arms. "These give me chill bumps. Last things she drew."

Sarah sniffles, and I admit these drawings make Leslie so much more real to me than even her picture in the news stories. Quietly I ask, "Do any of these people look familiar?"

We go through them again, but it's easy to see that it's all young people. Eden points at one. "That kind of looks like you, Sarah."

"I noticed that too," I say. I reach over and lay my hand on her shoulder. "Very pretty. Maybe we could frame it for you."

"She did say she was drawing me. She said drawing things helped her remember."

"Remember what?" I gently ask.

With a shrug she sighs, and it's a wobbly sigh. "She never said. I figure just stuff. People. Places. You know. But I don't know any of these people. Some of them look familiar, but it's no one I could name. They could've just been people on the beach and around the fort that day."

Eden leans over to hug Sarah. "I guess I should let Aiden know that we found this, right?"

"I think so," I agree. "Don't worry, Sarah, I'm sure they'll only take a look and then give it back to you. There's obviously no picture of her father here."

"Besides," Eden says as she begins to wad up the sandwich wrappers, "they know who her father is now."

"That's true," I say. With another squeeze of Sarah's shoulder, I stand up. "Having these pictures must be nice for you."

Eden whips around. "And don't let Mark or Miss Eustis try to claim them."

"Oh no." I tap my head with my fingers. "I forgot to tell you. Eustis is missing."

Sarah squints at me. "What? Missing how?"

Eden cocks her head. "Who told you that?"

"Annie Bryant. Mark got out of jail, and she wasn't at their house when he returned. No one knows where she is."

Eden's eyes narrow, and she shakes her head. "You ever seen that show *Swamp People*? Those folks that hunt alligators? Well, that's Miss Eustis and Mark. There's no need to worry about her. She can handle herself just fine."

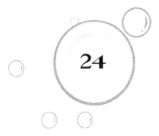

24

"I hope you understand," the older gentleman with the soft, Southern accent says, looking around at our little group. He meets each of our eyes, and we smile back at him. Annie reaches out and pats his hand. Tamela blushes, but Cherry squints and lifts her chin just a smidge. I nod at him, then look up at Lucy who stands beside him, patting his back.

Lucy was the one who brought him here—Leslie's father. Senator Stanford Little.

She'd sprung him on us as an old friend who needed to explain why he wanted us to stop asking questions—not to stop asking questions about the murder, but to realize he had nothing to do with it. He was only trying to bring his daughter into his family, and it all went horribly wrong.

He has nice, brown eyes; short, gray hair; and isn't someone you'd notice on the street. He has on khaki shorts and a yellow sports shirt. He's been retired from the state senate for a dozen years now. (I know because I googled him when I went to get him a glass of water.) He has two sons and a daughter. He actually choked up when he corrected himself. "No, I have two daughters." He tried to smile. "I was looking forward to saying that, but now…" He went on to tell his story, and now we're all sitting here letting the pizza get cold.

He puts his hands on his knees to stand up from the settee. "I should let you ladies get back to your dinner. I thank you, Lucy and Mrs. Mantelle especially, for letting me come talk to you. I was ready to welcome Leslie into my family. When I discovered she'd run out of my house on Sunday night, I decided that was her choice." He runs his tongue around the inside of his mouth as his eyes grow shiny. "I just thought we'd do it another time. I had no idea there wouldn't be another time."

I stand as he stands. "But you're sure she ran off to the south? Toward Peele's Point?"

"That's what I was told. I never actually saw her that evening." His voice catches and he swallows.

After a small pause, I soften my voice to ask, "But who told you that?"

"Not sure. You see, no one else knew who she was, so they weren't really paying attention to her, sad to say." Everyone is standing now, and we shuffle around a bit. Questioning people sure isn't easy.

Cherry clears her throat and asks, "I know you've already told us, but is it okay if I ask who all was there again?"

"Of course. My daughter Amelia and her husband, Ben; my son Richard; and his son, who is seven. My other son lives in Arizona, so he wasn't able to be here. I'd planned to tell him the next day; now I'm not sure if I should upset them all." He reaches out a hand to Lucy, which she grasps. "My friends know I was devastated when my wife, Therese, died of cancer at only forty-three. I avoided everything on the island, where we'd met, dated, had our three children, and lived our lives. The children were so young, all under twelve, but I had a lot of help with Therese's family nearby. I met Leslie's mother at a restaurant out near the interstate, and she was just so different from anyone in my world. As I said, she had no idea who I was or that I'd lost my wife. We were only together for a few weeks that summer. I knew she was married, and I'm ashamed to say it didn't matter. She helped me not think. But we knew it was just a fling, so then we went our separate ways." He looks at me. "And I agree with what your young friend said. Eustis can take care of herself. I'm sure she'll turn up in a day or two. She's not one to grieve in public."

Annie throws up her hands as she steps toward him. "I know you're a senator and all, but I have to give you a hug. You poor thing." She hugs him, and he hugs her back.

"Thank you. I appreciate your time, ladies, but I need to get back home." He turns and takes both of Lucy's hands in his own. "Thank you, Lucy, for reaching out to me. You're a dear friend."

She squeezes his hands, then steps toward the door. "Thank you, Stanford. You have a good evening, and I'll see you soon."

When the door is closed, no one says anything for a few moments.

Then Cherry says, "So that's Senator Little."

Tamela takes a deep breath. "Yep. I voted for him every time."

Annie and Lucy nod and say, "Me too."

Cherry looks at me, and we grimace a bit.

"I'll heat up the pizza if everyone's ready to eat," I say as I look around the room, but everyone still seems lost in their own thoughts.

"Sure. I'll help," Cherry says. But before she's halfway to the kitchen door she stops and shakes her head, looking at the floor. "First, though, I feel like I have to say I'm glad I never had the opportunity to vote for Senator Little. I'm, uh, I'm not sure I trust him."

Lucy, Annie, and Tamela's heads all jerk back. "Trust?" Lucy asks, and then they all burst out laughing. Cherry and I turn back to stare at them, then at each other in bewilderment.

Annie puts her arm around Lucy's neck. "You think her bringing him here had anything to do with her trusting him? Oh no, he's a snake in the grass from way back." She bends down to kiss her friend's cheek, leaving a bright red mark. "Lucy just knows that our Senator Little can't imagine that we common folk have his number. Makes him easy to get info out of. Now where's that hot pizza? I'm starving!"

Tamela wipes her hands with her napkin and puts her empty paper plate on the floor to the side of her chair. "Okay, do we add the senator to our suspect list?" she asks, opening her notepad.

We all nod.

Lucy folds her arms on the tops of her knees, wine glass in hand. "He's obviously in good enough health to have strangled her, especially if she thought she had nothing to fear from him. He hugs her, and…" She shudders.

Tamela writes as she says, "I've been thinking about it. The murder didn't have to be done at the same time she was buried. A body in the dunes and grasses wouldn't be seen in the dark. With so few people having beach lighting now due to the turtle regulations, there's not much light even outside of turtle season. Plus, I checked: there was not much of a moon that night."

"Oh, I see what you're saying," Annie says. "Yes, the murderer might go back later when there's no one around and make the fake nest."

"But why go back to the scene?" I reach over to grab a small piece of crust Lucy had cut off her slice and left in the box. "That's risking a lot if you've already gotten away with it."

Cherry stands up and begins collecting our empty plates. "I need more wine, anyone else? But it makes perfect sense to me. What if he hadn't gone back? First light of day, Leslie's body would have been discovered. The whole area would be cordoned off by the police, and a murder investigation would begin." She continues from the kitchen. "With the fake turtle nest excitement, everyone there erased any evidence and delayed the murder investigation for hours." She walks back in carrying the bottle and proceeds to fill our raised glasses.

"Rather ingenious if you think about it," Annie says with another of her trademark sighs. "Guess that's why I always had trouble believing it was Mark. Girls, he's my son-in-law, and he just ain't that smart. Take this whole thing with his momma being missing. Neighborhood kid shows up to feed the dogs this afternoon and says Miss Callahan called and asked him to do so until she called him back. Did Mark check with her neighbors about her missing? No. He just called a couple church friends."

"Any idea where she is?" I ask.

"No, but Willie Joe is ready to bust a blood vessel."

"Who's Willie Joe?" I ask.

The other four all say, "Funeral director."

Cherry laughs. "I obviously don't know him like everyone else does, but you can't live here long without hearing about Willie Joe and his funerals."

Lucy sniffs. "Funerals are a big deal around here. Willie Joe knows how things should be done."

Cherry's raised eyebrows show she felt the brushback. She crosses her arms, leans back, and brings her glass up to her mouth.

Tamela taps her notepad on her leg. "Okay, anything else? Jewel found what Leslie had been sketching on Sunday, and that's been turned over to the police. Anything else from Sarah?"

"Just that Sarah and Eden are pretty sure that Leslie wouldn't have anything to do with the group of college kids on the beach. They pointed out that she was found in the opposite direction of Peele's Point." I pause and look at our note taker. "Tamela, now that we're pretty sure Mark didn't do it, I'm still wondering why you were so adamant about his innocence from the very beginning."

She scribbles on her notepad a bit longer

than necessary so that by the time she softly answers, head still bowed, we're all watching her. "We moved here because of Hert's job with the paper mill, but we would've moved anywhere to get away from Alabama. I told you before that I trusted a student I shouldn't have, but it didn't end there." She looks up at us, dry-eyed but sad. "To make up for my misplaced trust in the student I became really too suspicious. I not only didn't trust anyone, but I was on the front line for judging. All because I'd been so embarrassed by my full support of the boy that had been guilty. Well, all my judging ended up with me helping get a fellow teacher fired. He was innocent, but that was discovered too late for his career and family to be put back together."

She stares past us, obviously replaying the event in her mind. Annie reaches over to pat her knee. "We all make mistakes, honey."

Tamela smiles at her, and her eyes focus. "I know. But most mistakes don't ruin people's lives." She takes a deep breath. "Anyway, I substituted out in Chambree a lot when we first moved here. I actually taught in Mark's high school, so I knew of him, but not well. I just didn't think he could kill his sister. Plus, I decided years ago it's better to err on the side of innocence than guilt."

Lucy drains the last sip of her wine. "I agree, but I still want to find the guilty person. Whoever killed Leslie Callahan deserves to be caught. However…"

Annie grimaces. "However, if it's Stanford Little, it'll be real hard to do. While we see through him, most men don't. He's a real guy's guy. Just look at how the police were willing to keep his name out of everything." She holds up her phone like we can read the text from our seats. "Aiden says everyone at the station is furious that we all know about the senator."

Lucy throws up a hand at her friend. "Men. They think they can keep secrets."

We hear steps on the front porch and turn that way as the door opens. Eden's eyes are larger than usual as she stage-whispers, "Officer Greyson is behind me. He's mad."

Sure enough, with a quick knock on the already open door, Officer Greyson strides into the room. He nods to Eden and then looks around at the rest of us. "Ladies." He turns toward me. "Mrs. Mantelle, can I have a word with you? Maybe out back?"

He holds out his arm in that direction, and with a look at my friends, I lead him down the hallway to the back door.

Greyson takes my elbow, and we walk

out onto the uneven brick path, away from the house. The setting sun fills the yard with shafts of orange light and deep shadows. We only go about ten yards before we stop and I can turn to get a better look at his face. Eden's right. He does look mad.

Then he grins. "Okay, what did Stanford Little have to say?"

25

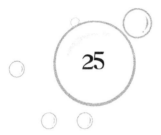

"Aren't you furious with us for knowing that he's Leslie's father?" His grin has me thrown off. I fold my arms and tip my chin up to show him that I don't care if he's furious.

His grin only grows. He relaxes, shuffling his feet and then shrugging.

"Wait," I say. "You wanted us to talk to him."

He squints at me, but his grin stays in place.

Seeing my friends' faces lurking in the back window of Craig's office, I smirk and tell Greyson, "Good thing you're facing this way with that ridiculous grin. We have an audience."

"Why do you think I'm facing this way?

You can keep facing them, but try to look mad." He shifts his stance and pulls out his notebook and pen. "The worst part of this is that I can't involve Aiden, so I have to take my own notes. I'm not allowed to talk to the *esteemed* senator, so what did he tell y'all?"

Keeping my face serious, I hurry through the highlights and conclude by telling him we don't believe Senator Little.

Nodding, he says, "Good for you."

"Then why did everyone vote for him? I still don't get it."

"He ran unopposed for the most part. Plus, he may have been a rat, but he was *our* rat. Better than someone else's. And not everybody distrusted him. Some people like rats." He practically spits that last part out. Placing his pen on his paper, he asks, "Anything else?"

I smile as Cherry holds up a glass of wine, mimicking drinking it all in one swallow. Officer Greyson smiles, and when my eyes slide back to him, my smile grows before I can remember. Stop this, I tell myself. He's a married man. Oh, and I'm a married woman.

He starts to turn, but I reach out and grab his forearm. "Wait." He turns to me. "We think the murder and the hiding in the fake nest might have happened at different times."

He nods, then hangs his thumbs in his belt, and my hand drops off his arm. I'm shocked to find I'd left it there that long.

"That fits with what we were thinking. However, you can't underestimate how badly folks want this to just go away." He takes a deep breath. "I can't believe I resorted to leaving clues for Lucy and now questioning you." His eyes flick up at me. "Oh, and Lucy doesn't know I left the clues. I used one of the dispatchers she volunteers with. Plus, I figure y'all being out in the open with your investigating is one of the best ways to ensure your safety."

"I don't think anyone is paying any attention to us," I say. "So, is that all? You want a piece of pizza?" We begin walking back to the house, the faces in the window long gone.

"No, thanks. Heading home for dinner." He opens the back door, then steps down to let go inside. "Ladies first."

I bend my head toward his and whisper, "Can I tell them?"

He shakes his head. "It's better if we keep it just between us that we're working together."

I swallow and dash up the steps. We were standing just a tad too close.

Officer Greyson apparently left around the back of the house after I hurried inside. As I come into the living room, all evidence of our pizza party is gone and the ladies seated around the room greet me with solemn stares. Annie winks and pats the cushion beside her. "Come tell us what Charlie wanted."

"Why do you guys look so serious?" I take my seat beside Annie, and she pats my thigh, then nods at Lucy.

Petite, golden-haired Lucy clears her throat. "He wanted to know about the senator, didn't he?"

"Maybe."

Lucy give me that mothering look that says, "I will find out, so just go ahead and tell me." It doesn't help that, as I look around the room, I find that same look on all my friends' faces.

"Okay, so what if he did? He needs our help."

Cherry shakes her head. "He didn't ask for our help. He asked for your help."

"What? Now no one trusts Officer

Greyson? Hello? Annie, he's your son's partner."

She sighs. "I know, and it just kills me but, well, the girls are right. He might not be able to be trusted in this particular matter."

Lucy rolls her eyes. "Well, it doesn't kill me! He used that silly dispatcher that flits around playing volunteer at the chamber to lead me right to Stanford. He used her, and he used me and my friendship with the Littles." She settles herself and folds her arms into a hard knot.

I stare at her. How did she know that?

Cherry throws up her hands at me. "Oh, great. She's not denying it. Come on, what did he say?"

"I'm confused. When did Charlie Greyson become the bad person here?" I close my eyes and shake my head as I capitulate. "He can't interview the senator, so he needed a little help. He trusts me. Us."

Tamela is scribbling on her notepad, and she mumbles, "You. He trusts you." She looks up at me and gives me a tiny, cynical smile. "'Cause you're new here."

"So?" I ask. Annie leans away from me to put her phone in her pocket and then gets up off the settee.

She says, "I've got to go. Amber needs me to help get the kids in bed. Mark's been over to see them, and he always gets them all ramped up." She stops and places a hand on Lucy's shoulder. "Tell her."

Lucy nods. Charlie has an ax to grind with the senator, so maybe he's leading the blame in that direction. He set me up to bring Stanford over here, using the fact that none of us trust him as far as we can throw him." Her cheeks grow pink, and she presses her lips together for a moment. "I kind of understand it, but I hate to be treated like an idiot. I hate it even more when I *act* like an idiot! Running straight to the Littles' house and dragging Stanford over here. Charlie Greyson is going to get a piece of my mind the next time I see him!"

Lucy is usually the very picture of genteel Southern womanhood, but she's really hot under the collar right now. I guess this is what it looks like when a mature Southern belle has had her bell rung.

Cherry's eyes are as wide as mine. Annie is actually laughing but standing well out of sight behind her friend as Lucy rants on.

Finally Tamela slams her notebook down on the coffee table in front of her. "Lucy! Get a hold of yourself. He didn't frame you and throw you in jail!" With a sigh she turns to me, and finally I get some answers. "Charlie's wife is one of the senator's long-time girlfriends."

"What? Really?"

They all nod at me.

I add, "Like now…?"

This time their nods are a little wiggly, and Tamela adds a half-hearted shrug.

Annie pulls her pocketbook strap over her shoulder. "We put it all together while you two were out there flirting." She turns to struggle with opening the front door. "The senator was the topic of your conversation, right?"

"Right."

Tamela picks up her notebook. "We got to thinking that someone could be trying to set Stanford up. What if one of his girlfriends thought he was serious about Leslie? They would have no idea he was her daughter." She shows me the list of names they'd been working on.

"That many? And everyone knows?" I exclaim.

Lucy stands and sighs. "He's lived here a long time, been widowed a long time, and it's a really small island."

Annie suddenly jerks the big front door open. We all stand, but we move slowly, everyone deep in their own thoughts.

Cherry stops at the edge of the front porch steps. "I thought we'd pretty much solved this. Senator Little just seemed so, so perfect to be guilty."

Nodding, I pat her on the back, and she walks on down.

Tamela is the only one left on the porch with me. "We're going to look into a couple of women the senator has been with recently, but it seems like kind of a stretch. A jealous husband setting him up by murdering a girl on the beach? More likely it was a jealous woman, but the police said it was a man."

"Or a woman with large hands," I remind her.

"You keep talking to the police and see what you can find out. Even with all those people giving the senator an alibi, I still think he's our best bet." She hikes her large purse over her shoulder and jogs down the steps. "Lucy's going to look into the family, see if those alibis are any good."

On the ground she turns around. "Hey, the house is looking better. Looks like lots of trimming got done," she says as she surveys the thick blanket of cut branches surrounding the walkway. "Thanks for having us over. See you later," she shouts with a wave, getting in her car.

Tamela turns around to pull out of the driveway, and then she's on the road and out of sight. As the yard grows still, the frogs and bugs fill the emptiness, though it never really feels empty here. Moving from the northwest in winter, where there are only bare fields and bare trees, when everything feels laid out and exposed, makes Florida feel full. Full of noise, plants, birds—even the air feels full. At home we'd look eagerly for the first leaves and first plants popping through the snow, finally announcing winter's end, like dressing for a special event, each adornment anticipated and celebrated. We'd revel in the opening and blossoming as they wiped away the memories of bareness. But here? Here, it's like crowding more people into an already full elevator. There is absolutely no more room, and yet…

Lush. Lavish. Sated. It's more than just the heat that slows things here. At the top of the steps I turn and look around the yard, the porch, and then through the front windows to the softly lit living room. Then I realize, as strange as it seems here at times, I feel like I'm home.

Home. The word settles inside me as I move indoors and pick up my phone. I guess the sooner I tell Craig the better.

26

"Get dressed. Nice, but not fancy," Lucy says as soon as I press the green answer button on my phone at eight a.m.

"For what?" I am dressed, but for some reason I don't believe the elastic-waist shorts and an old T-shirt from Erin's high school track team are fancy enough for whatever Lucy has in mind.

"I'm picking you up in thirty minutes. We're going to see Amelia Little, Stanford's daughter, about the Christmas home tour. She's on the committee."

"Christmas tour? It's barely spring, and besides, why am I going?"

"You're the ticket in to see her. Getting the Mantelle house on the tour would be an incredible feather in her cap, so she said for us to come right over. We've been working on the final list of houses for weeks now. And this isn't early; it's almost too late for changes."

"Oh." I look around the yard, where I'm making piles of trimmed branches. Eden's father, Ted, is out of town for a few days, and I don't know the tree trimmer's name. I thought the air was full last night, but I had no idea what it would feel like after actually working out in it. "It may take more than thirty minutes. I'm soaked with sweat, so I have to take a shower."

She says, "Okay," hanging up before she gets the whole word out.

I've got stuff to do, and this detective thing feels like a giant goose chase. I pull off my gloves and lay them on the porch railing to dry as I walk into the house. Us solving the murder last month was most likely a fluke, and besides, I'm tired of thinking about something so sad. Leslie was younger than my girls. What if some vagrant did kill her? What if there is nothing to discover? What if we're just harassing innocent people? What if Officer Greyson *is* looking for evil on the part of a man he rightfully despises?

However, if it gets me out of doing yardwork in this humidity, then I say let's go do some detecting!

"In my next life I'm coming back tall and thin so I can wear dresses like that," Lucy says as I open her passenger side door and slide into the seat, searching for the seat belt.

"Are you joking? You always look so put together, so stylish." I smooth down the new turquoise paisley dress I bought last week at Talbot's. It's a sleeveless sheath dress, and this is the first time I've worn it. "People wear a lot more dresses down here, I've noticed."

"Really? I didn't know that. I figured up north they dress more professionally than we do down here. Like on *The Real Housewives of New York*."

I laugh. "Well, that's not exactly the Midwest, where we're from. I also never worked in downtown Chicago, or in business. Anyway, before we get there, what exactly are we doing?"

"Talking to Amelia Little Perkins basically. I'd love it if we could clear Stanford from everybody's suspicions, but he's put himself in this position by being a cheater, first of all, but also by not telling everyone about Leslie. He wanted the big production of introducing her at a family dinner." She looks over at me and rolls her eyes. "Just like a politician, I guess. The more drama, the better."

"And you don't think it's possible he killed her?"

She purses her lips and shakes her head. "I don't. There wouldn't be any reason to call attention to her if he didn't want to claim her. Plus, he's not a very passionate man, except in the bedroom, I guess. He's very cool, almost cold. Him flying into a rage over something she said just doesn't feel right." Her mouth hangs open. I can see she's got something else to say, so I wait. "Plus, he's very much a schemer, a planner. Him changing his mind about announcing she's his daughter isn't likely. He'd have thought it all through. Matter of fact, that's what made me think of calling Amelia. She's very much like him, so offering her your house plays to two of her weaknesses: scheming and winning."

She turns onto A1A, and it strikes me all over again that the ocean is right there behind the houses. I look for glimpses of it as we drive south on the island. "They live near you, right?" The ladies had made the connection for me last night that Stanford Little's daughter is married to the Benjamin involved with the turtles and that they were the couple we saw having the photo session on the beach.

"Yes, only a couple houses down on the other side of the beach access. Their careers are obviously taking off because the house wasn't in Amelia's family." Lucy shrugs and leans toward me, also flicking her eyes in my direction. "And Benjamin's family, I hear, is *not* well off."

"He won't be there, will he?"

"Hopefully not. I'll take all the help in the world for the turtles, but he's using them to further his political future. I just know it." She pulls into the driveway of a beautiful home, which is accented by a wide flight of white stairs leading up to massive double doors painted a rich coral. A landscaped lawn, perfect palm trees, and flowers swaying in the ocean breeze welcome us as she parks on the expanse of pavers, which make a very elegant driveway/front yard combination.

Whereas Lucy and her mother's home looks like an authentic beach house, this feels like something out of a magazine.

"Did they build this?" I ask as we get out of the car.

"No, it was just like ours, but it was flipped a few years ago." She comes close to me. "Its value now is close to three million."

"I don't think I've ever been in a three-million-dollar house." I am very glad I wore my new dress.

Lucy winks at me. "Keep traveling with me, kid, and you'll see grander places than this!" She laughs and heads up the front stairs. "Amelia works from home, and as impressed as you are by this house, yours is the mystery house, the one she'd love to be able to say she got for the Christmas home tour." She rings the doorbell, then whispers from behind her hand, "So play hard to get."

The door begins to open, and Lucy's smile widens as her accent thickens. "Hey there, oh—Benjamin."

"Hello, Mrs. Fellows, Mrs. Mantelle. Good to see you again so soon. Come in." He opens the door wide, and white-tiled floors lead to a wall of windows overlooking the ocean. There's furniture and carpets in the way, but the morning sun shines on the floors just as brightly as it is on the water and the sand beyond the windows, making it all look like one expanse of light.

"This is beautiful," I say in awe, stepping around Lucy.

Benjamin turns to take a few steps with me. "Isn't it? When I'm late to the office it's because I find it impossible to pull myself away." He laughs and asks, "Can I get you ladies a cup of coffee? Anything?" He's wearing a suit, but his tie is only draped around his neck and he's barefoot. "Amelia will be right down."

Lucy speaks up. "Coffee would be wonderful. I take mine black."

I ask for some water, and he directs us to the seating area near the windows. Lucy sits immediately on the navy couch, but I walk over to the windows and realize they are wall-sized sliding doors. "This whole thing slides away? How wonderful is that?"

Lucy grimaces. "Every time I'm in one of these flipped houses I get almost sick to my stomach. This is what our house could look like if we actually had any money."

"But I love your house. It's perfect for you and your mother." I check around, then whisper, "Much homier."

Benjamin brings our drinks, and then as he knots his tie he asks about Lucy's mother, Birdie. It makes me wonder if he heard us talking.

"She's fine. Just getting older, but I suppose we all are." Lucy picks up her cup but tips her head to look up at him. "Your father-in-law, however, seems to be getting younger at times. Doesn't it seem that way to you? I saw him yesterday. He said he got to have dinner with the family Sunday?"

Pausing in the act of pulling his tie tight, Benjamin furrows his brow in thought. "Sunday? We drove back from Atlanta, oh, Sunday night. Yes. Richard and Barlow were in town, and Stanford wanted to have us all together." He looks over at me. "You're not from here. Richard is Amelia's brother, and Barlow is his son. They live in Jacksonville."

"Nice to have everyone so close. All four of my kids live in the Midwest."

"Amelia's other brother lives in Arizona." He finishes off his tie with a gentle push, then sits down where I notice his socks and shoes are waiting for him.

Lucy asks, "Is your family from around here?"

He laughs as he pulls on a sock. "Oh, no, ma'am. Up in Georgia, almost to the Tennessee line. I didn't even see the ocean until Amelia brought me here when we were almost done with law school." He shakes his head as he slides his feet into his shoes. "Never imagined I'd live beside it."

Lucy leans forward. "Your parents didn't like the ocean? I hear there are folks like that."

"Yeah, I guess," he mumbles, his face turned toward the floor as he ties his shoes.

"Sorry you had to wait!" Amelia exclaims, running down the wide open staircase.

Benjamin jumps up. "Amelia, slow down! You scare me to death the way you run down those stairs." He meets her at the bottom and kisses her.

She snuggles against him. "Silly man, I always hold on to the railing. I know I'm a little front heavy these days."

I step toward her, but she meets me more than halfway. She looks like she belongs in this sun-filled castle beside the sea. Her blonde hair curls halfway down her back, and her face is as open as the view. Her shirt is long and flowing and looks like the inside of a seashell in shimmering pink and peach. Her white pants are silk and yet do not look like pajamas. "Mrs. Mantelle, it's so wonderful to have you here," she says. "I don't believe we've met."

"No. We did spy on your photo shoot, though, so I feel like I know you."

Concern crosses her face, and she looks up at her husband, then back at me. "Photo shoot?"

Lucy stands as she says, "On the beach. You were right in front of my house and I had the ladies over for supper."

"Oh, that's right," Amelia says, then titters. "Miss Lucy, so good to see you again. How's Miss Birdie? I need to stop in and see her."

"She would love that."

Then the conversation dies, like when you're blowing a bubble and it pops.

The others look like they want to say something. Me? I'm just along for the ride, so I turn to look out the window again.

Benjamin speaks up. "I need to get to work. Mrs. Fellows, I hope you're not too upset about the whole turtle thing." He shrugs and continues, "But you've got to admit it could really be done better with more cooperation and coordination across the state."

Lucy pulls her shoulders back. "I believe we do just fine here on Sophia."

He reaches a hand out, his dark eyes wide and his hair bouncing a bit on his forehead as he takes a step toward her. "Oh, I agree. Wholeheartedly agree! You are a shining example to the entire state. If only we could clone you!" He takes her hand in both of his. "I'm afraid Sheila Hornsby's rough-around-the-edges demeanor has soured waters between you and me. We can, and should, work together."

Lucy doesn't exactly melt. That said, I've never seen her melt and I'm not sure what it would look like, so maybe what she's doing *is* melting. It's definitely blushing. Lucy Fellows is blushing. I feel like I should be recording this.

"Oh, Benjamin. I'm so happy to hear you say this. Let's do try to work together. It's all about the turtles."

"Yes, ma'am." His smile is full of relief, and he actually reaches over to hug her.

Amelia claps her hands. "I told him you are just one of the sweetest ladies on this entire island and he *must* find a way to work with you. Must get on your good side."

He lets go of Lucy, then leans over to side-hug and kiss his wife. "I have to leave. Mrs. Fellows, we will talk. Soon."

Heading out through the kitchen he shouts, "Goodbye!"

Amelia spreads her arms toward the couch and chairs. "Please sit. Miss Lucy, I'm so glad that turtle thing is settled. I told Benjamin I simply would not have him being on your bad side. Simply would not have it." She winks at us from the high-back chair she floated into. "Daddy told him that also. No one crosses Daddy's friends." She turns to me and claps her hands. "Now. About the home tour."

Lucy grabs the conversation back. "Jewel met your father yesterday. How does that man stay so good-looking?"

Amelia's face lights up, which hardly seems possible as she was already glowing. "Daddy is a miracle, isn't he? He was a senator, did Miss Lucy tell you that? Where did y'all run into him? He's been so busy lately I can't hardly get a minute of his time." She looks at me, but I have no idea what yarn Lucy plans to spin, so I take a long drink of water.

"Oh, just here and there," Lucy says with a flick of her hand. Then she leans forward and lowers her voice. "He was rather sad to hear that the woman who was killed had been at his house Sunday evening, same as y'all."

"At Daddy's house? I don't think so. We were there, but no one else. I mean outside family."

I choke on my water, and they both look at me, Lucy with sternness, Amelia with concern as she asks, "Are you okay?"

Lucy punctuates her perturbed look with, "She's fine. Anyway, you don't remember anyone else being in the house? Possibly in the kitchen?" She lifts her hands in question. "Leslie was definitely there. Your father said y'all even saw her leaving on the beach."

Amelia rubs her belly and thinks. "I don't think so." Then her eyebrows lift and she says with certainty, "No, the girl on the beach was only twenty-five. There was a woman helping in the kitchen, but she was much older."

So what I'd seen in the newspaper's pictures was true in real life. Leslie's lifestyle had aged her.

Lucy speaks up. "Yes. That was her. Leslie Callahan. She left before, well, before y'all had dinner."

Amelia shakes her head, then suddenly stops. "Are you sure? But why would she leave if she was supposed to help with dinner? You say Daddy saw her leave?"

Lucy gives me a questioning look. I shake my head and say, "I don't think he said he saw her, but someone in your family saw her walking down toward Peele's Point."

"So that really was her? Oh, that's awful." She pulls her fist to her mouth and her eyes grow shiny. "So we were, like, some of the last people to see her alive? Well, except for the person who killed her."

"Man," Lucy corrects. "It was a *man* that killed her. The handprints were too large to be a woman's."

"Her brother, right?" Amelia chews on

her lip, then draws in a long breath like her stomach is queasy.

"Doesn't look like it," Lucy forges on. "Did you actually talk to her at your dad's?"

Holding her mouth shut and breathing through her nose—attempting to keep her breakfast down, I'm sure—Amelia shakes her head. "No. I came in alone and saw her in the kitchen as I passed by. I, uh, thought she was helping out. Daddy's chef was there, and sometimes he hires extra help. But, you know, her dress…" Amelia's eyebrows flattens as she concentrates. "I do remember thinking she wasn't dressed to serve. It was a nice dress. Pink."

"Who else was there?" Lucy asks, leaning forward.

"Daddy was somewhere in the house. I think his room. Barlow and Richard were playing a video game in the living room, and Benjamin was still outside. He was rolling up the garden hose that the gardener had left lying in the driveway. I hurried on into the living room to see Richard and my nephew, and I guess that's when she left." She stands up. "I need a drink of water. Anything else for you ladies?" She smiles, but it's a sick smile and she presses on her stomach with her hand.

She takes several deep breaths, and her color comes back and her face relaxes.

"You poor thing," Lucy says as we also stand and follow Amelia into the kitchen. "What an awful subject for us to bring up. We came to talk about the Christmas house tour and somehow ended up on such a distasteful topic."

"Oh, that's right!" Amelia's face lights back up. "Mrs. Mantelle, we'd so love to have your home on our tour. It would be the crown jewel even in its current state." She stops at the kitchen island and turns to me, taking my hand. "Please say yes."

Now my stomach feels a little queasy, but following her example I take a deep breath, smile, and say, "Yes, but—"

My 'yes' is all she needs, as her words bubble out and all over the room. "And now that I've seen you I know the house will be just as classy and put together as you are. I can't wait to see it." She swirls toward her huge, wood-paneled refrigerator. "I'll get all the information on the photo shoot and advertising to you soon. I'd like to have all that nailed down before the baby comes."

The mother-to-be is pouring a glass of water, so she doesn't see the horrified look I give Lucy, which my friend dismisses with a sniff and a turn toward the front door. "Yes, that all sounds wonderful. Amelia, darling, you have a good morning. Jewel and I need to be on our way."

Lucy and I meander down the stairs after a round of hugs and goodbyes. On the front landing, Amelia stands in the open doorway, the sunlight from inside the house shining around her. Lucy shades her eyes as she turns more fully back. "One more question. How was the food? At dinner Sunday?"

Amelia looks confused, then smiles. "Oh, wonderful. Daddy always hires Miss Tunney for family meals. You know she worked for us for years after Mommy died. I always called her Miss Funny. It was a wonderful night—" Then she catches herself. "I mean, well, it was for us, but not…"

"It's okay, sweetie," Lucy says. Then she turns down the stairs. "We know."

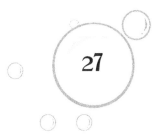

27

"I don't think Amelia had any idea who Leslie was. That she was there to be introduced as her sister. Do you?" Lucy asks me as she pulls out to drive down the oceanfront highway.

"No," I say. "But doesn't her lack of curiosity seem a bit strange? Think about it. There's this young woman at your father's house when you arrive, then she just disappears and no one says anything about it?" I have to yell since Lucy lowered the top on her convertible. I can't see anything with my hair blowing everywhere. I continue yelling, "She acted like she hadn't put together that the dead girl and the girl at the house were one and the same."

"That's really not so unusual knowing

Stanford as I do. He very easily ignores what he doesn't want to see. And Amelia is very much like her father," Lucy says with a raise of her eyebrows in my direction.

Holding my hair back, I can see her mouth presses into a frown, a deep frown, which kept trying to show up while we were speaking with Amelia Little Perkins. I'm not sure if it's that the women grew up here so people know them by their maiden names or if it's a Southern thing that so many are called by two last names. I know having two first names is Southern, but this? I'm not sure where it comes from, but now they've got me doing it. Anyway, Lucy looks like she doesn't quite buy the story that the Sunday night dinner at the senator's went as smoothly as we're being told.

Lucy's and my thoughts must be on the same page. Just as I remember Amelia saying that, Lucy says, "I bet the police haven't even talked to Tunney. Get my phone. See if I have her in my contacts."

She presses the button to unlock it when I hold it out to her, then I ask, "How do you spell it? T-U-N…"

"Yes. It sounds like 'funny,' but with an 'E-Y' on the end. She's as old as my mother but still just as strong as an ox. Cooks for the restaurant Miss Christine's most mornings and apparently does family meals for Stanford."

"Here it is. Want me to call her?"

After a pause while she chews her bottom lip, Lucy looks at me, lifting her sunglasses. "Have you had breakfast?"

Miss Christine's is an unassuming restaurant in a strip mall on one of the main roads, but it's an institution on Sophia Island. Apparently Miss Christine's was around for years in another location and opened here a few years ago. Its proximity to the beach hotels means a steady flow of new customers, but apparently the locals love it too. I say this because both times Craig and I tried to get in on a weekend morning there was a long line. Craig does not believe in waiting in line.

When I worry about the line, though, Lucy flutters her hand at me. "Oh, fiddle-faddle. They seat folks fast, and besides, you always know people in line to talk to!"

I do not believe that line of logic would've changed Craig's mind.

Annie often says Lucy flits around. Watching her enter Miss Christine's, I have to agree that the verb "flit" works. She knows every other person, waiters included. They all have to hug her, she has to ask about their momma, they have to ask about her momma, and then they move on, often carrying armloads of hot dishes. I hear her mention Tunney's name a couple times, and then before I know it Lucy's flitting across the room and motioning for me to follow her. She claims a small table for four and plops down. "See? That didn't take any time!"

"I didn't see a menu."

"You'll get one." She winks at me. "But you don't need one. I can tell you what to get."

"What? Biscuits and gravy? You turning into Annie now?"

She unwraps her utensils. "Hush your mouth. Annie is pushy. I'm beguiling. Seductive. Enticing." She winks again and laughs.

I can't help but laugh too. "Honestly, Lucy, I've never seen anyone feed off people like you do." Her quick frown tells me to backtrack. "Not in a bad way! You just love people, and it's obvious. You, ah, they power you."

She adds a little pout to her frown. "Maybe. I've never thought about it. I do like people, though." She lights up. "You should've seen my mother in her heyday. She lit up city blocks with her charm. It's sad her being cooped up in that house so much, but she says she's happiest there. Says being out and about wears her out."

A large, black lady wearing an official-looking apron and plastic hairnet approaches our table. She reaches down and hugs Lucy from behind. "There's my sugar. Where's your momma? You've got to bring her down to see me. I'd make a fresh batch of cinnamon rolls just for her." She pulls away from Lucy, but only to sit down with us.

"Tunney, darlin'," Lucy begins, "we were just talking about Miss Birdie. She sure would love to see you." She grabs the woman's large hand and squeezes it, then nods at me. "This here is my friend Jewel."

Clucking her tongue, Tunney rears back. "Aw, Mrs. Mantelle. You are just as fresh as a daisy like I heard. Where you from now?"

"Chicago. All over the Midwest, really. It's nice to meet you."

"You as well. Everybody is talking about your house being on the home tour. Them tickets will sell out as fast as they print them," she says, reaching over to nudge my arm.

"But… how?" I stammer.

Lucy just rolls her eyes at me. She focuses on Tunney. "Amelia called you?"

"Mm, nope. Not doing it." Her plastic cap crinkles as she shakes her head from side to side. "Lucy, girl, I'm not telling tales from Mr. Little's. Not doing it."

Lucy is persistent. She leans in close. "Was Leslie Callahan helping you Sunday night? The girl is dead, Tun."

Raising one eyebrow so far it disappears behind her plastic cap, Tunney speaks out of one side of her mouth, as though if she doesn't open her whole mouth she's not actually saying anything. "She didn't look like no girl. That one has been rode hard and put up wet." Her shoulders fall. "But still too young to die like that. Buried in the sand." She shudders.

"Did you talk to her at all?"

"Nope." She pushes herself out of her chair. "She came into the kitchen, happy as a lark. Called me by name, but I was concentrating on putting some garnishes on my deviled eggs. Those are Richard's favorite and his boy, Barlow, can eat a plate by himself." She grins for a moment, then sighs. "I didn't even look up. When I'm working in folks' homes, it doesn't always pay to notice things." She twists her mouth and gives Lucy a look that says, "You know what I mean?"

"Especially not in Stanford's house, right?" Lucy whispers.

"You're right on that one." Tunney stands, then slides her chair back under the table. "She opened the back door out of the kitchen, and I looked up to see her going out and never thought another thought about it till I saw that picture in the newspaper."

Lucy gasps. "So you knew it was Leslie there that night?"

"What does that matter? She was a wild one, I hear. She was down with those crazy kids and was probably drunk or high. Her dying didn't have anything to do with me. Or Mr. Little."

"But you said she left out the kitchen door. You didn't see her go toward Peele's Point? Who did see her go that direction?" Lucy presses her lips together in frustration. "The kitchen is on the opposite side of the house from the point, Tunney."

Tunney leans over to whisper. "So? Maybe Mr. Little saw her going in that direction later. Who knows? I just know I don't want to be involved. You know everything I know."

"Shouldn't someone tell the police?" Lucy whispers back.

The tall woman leans back and stands straight as she shakes her head, then shrugs.

Tunney stares at her old friend, then nods at me. "Nice to meet you, Mrs. Mantelle. Good luck with the house tour. Lucy, I'll see you soon. Tell Birdie to come see me." She walks through the tables to the back.

Lucy gives me a sad smile, then waves at the waitress she'd turned away while Tunney was at our table.

As I watch the waitress spin on a dime toward our table, I ask, "Are you going to tell the police?"

She sighs. "I'm betting a whole tray of biscuits and a pot of gravy they already know."

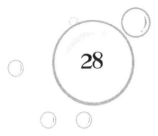

28

"Usually when I order an omelet I'm disappointed after eating it," I say, leaning back in my chair for our waitress to take my empty plate. "But not this time. That was amazing. So fresh!"

"Yes, ma'am," the waitress says. "All the vegetables are fresh every time, and the crab looked really good this morning. Anything else for you ladies?"

Lucy tips her coffee cup and looks into it. "I'll take a bit more coffee and a piece of coconut cake to go. Oh, and the check, please." She winks at me. "Breakfast is my treat for dragging you around and making you sign up for the home tour."

"You don't have to do that. As for the

tour, I'm sure it'll be no big deal. Is the coconut cake that good? I've seen several other people taking pieces home."

Lucy nods. "Old-fashioned recipe and huge pieces. You are oh so wrong about the home tour, but you have, what, six months to worry about that."

"Six? December is eight months out."

Lucy smirks at me. "You're cute. It takes at least two months of active planning and meetings to put this whole thing together in the fall." She looks around the room and spots our waitress. "Tiffany, another piece of coconut cake, please." She pulls her credit card out of her wallet and says to me, "You'll love it. It's a perfect treat for a Friday night. Don't argue! I owe you big time, and you'll have no idea just how much until December. So, will Craig be coming home to help you eat that piece of cake?" She keeps looking at things in her wallet like she didn't just ask about my MIA husband.

"No. We tried to talk last night, but we're at an impasse. He sees no need to come home before Memorial Day when the kids will be here."

That gets her to look up. "But that's over a month away! Davis has only been gone this week, and I can't wait to see him." She holds a hand over her mouth. "Oh, I'm sorry. I shouldn't say stuff like that."

"No." I tug on her arm to pull her hand away from her mouth, and I laugh a little. "I'm glad you're happy. I'm coming to see that I don't think we were ever very happy as a couple. As a family? We were pretty good, I think. Four kids close in age demands so much attention, and I just don't think I realized he and I didn't connect. He traveled all the time, and well, I don't remember missing him." With a sigh, I enjoy the feeling of release. Trying to act like I miss Craig has been exhausting. "I know I should miss him, being here by myself, but…" I shrug and smile. "Honestly, I don't."

"Do you think you'll divorce?"

"I don't know. I mean, I'm living in the family home he inherited only a few months ago. What happens to all that? I think he wants us to just keep existing the way we are, and I guess I can't figure out why we shouldn't."

The waitress sets two see-through containers holding humongous pieces of coconut cake on the table, then lays the check beside Lucy's hand. "You ladies have a good rest of your day."

Lucy looks at the check, slides her card

into the slot, and closes it. Her newly warmed coffee is steaming, so she moves it in front of her. She absently watches our waitress make her way back to take the check holder and card, and then she leans forward on her elbows. "But what if you meet someone?"

"Me?" I laugh. "I've never been good that, and I've realized working to make someone else comfortable and happy is not as much fun as when I was younger."

Lucy wrinkles her nose. "Well, of course not. But what about if someone comes along who wants to make *you* comfortable and happy? Men like that are out there, you know."

"Not interested." Then, with a scrunch of my nose, I laugh. "Give me a break. I just learned how to have female friends!"

Lucy leans back and takes the check holder as it's returned to her. "Okay, you're probably right. Just let things happen with you and Craig. One more question: any chance he finds someone or has found someone?"

"Absolutely not. He told me as much last night."

She cocks her head. "He told you? Or did you ask him and then he answered you?"

"Lucy! I would never ask him something like that." I sputter the water I was trying to drink and shake my head as I wipe my mouth. "Never. He's just not like that. He's into his work."

"Okay." She proceeds to put her card away, apply lipstick by looking in her phone's selfie camera—a tip I'm filing away for later, and take one last sip of coffee.

It's like she's daring me to continue this conversation, to ask what she meant by her question, but I don't want to know. I stand and push my chair in. "That was delicious. Thank you so much for breakfast"—I pick up my piece of cake—"and for dinner. See? Living alone has its perks."

Midmorning heat presses in on me as we walk to the car. "I'm working on getting used to this humidity, but it's something else."

Lucy agrees, but adds, "Davis was in Chicago this week, and he had to wear a coat. I'll take the humidity any day. And look at that cute dress you get to wear already."

"That's true. I wouldn't be wearing this back home in April without a sweater. How long have you and Davis been an item?"

"A little over ten years," she says, then sighs. We get into the car. "We both lost spouses. We actually met in a grief group at the Episcopal church."

"Oh, I'm sorry. I didn't realize that."

She smiles at me, then starts the car. "No

worries. Here, can you hold my cake too? Drop you off at your house?"

"Sure." We're out on the road before I add, "I look forward to meeting Davis. I'm glad you two are happy."

"Thanks. And we are happy. I need to live with Mother for now, though, and he travels a lot for work. We enjoy our lives, separately and together. My husband died suddenly, and it's been hard to get past."

"Oh, Lucy! I didn't know—"

"That's okay. Let's not talk about it now." She smiles and speeds up, the noise and wind helping us not talk.

Thinking of the relationships around me here on Sophia, I don't think Craig and I are that out of place. People are making things work. Without kids to raise, things can flow as needed. So much to think about, but for now I'm enjoying a seaside ride on a beautiful morning in a convertible.

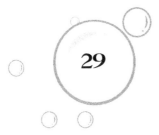

29

I walk into the house to find Aiden and Eden at the kitchen table eating an early lunch.

Eden starts talking with her mouth half full. "Dad says he'll have the tree guy back over here this week at the very latest." She swallows. "He says they'll take care of everything, no problem."

"This week? Today is Friday. Does he mean this week or next week?"

She thinks for a moment, eats another chip, and looks out the window for a moment. "His exact words were, 'This week at the very latest, but if that doesn't work out, then next week definitely.'"

Her innocent grin says she didn't actually hear the words she just said. A glance at Aiden says that he did. However, he only shrugs, grins, and points to the cake in my hand. "You went to Miss Christine's?"

"Yes," I answer as I walk to the refrigerator. "Lucy and I went to talk to Miss Tunney. You guys know her, I guess?" They nod as I come to the table and sit down. "Aiden, do the police know she saw Leslie the night she was murdered?"

Eden exclaims, "What!" and Aiden rolls his eyes.

"Of course we do, Miss Jewel. What do y'all think we're doing? Just sitting around eating donuts?"

Eden demands, "Where did Miss Tunney see Leslie?"

Aiden holds a hand up at us. "Privileged information! She didn't talk to her, and all she adds to the story is that Miss Callahan left the property. Correct, Miss Jewel?"

"Yeah, I guess that's right. But she didn't say Leslie went toward all the college kids."

Aiden dismisses that issue with just a wave of his hand. "She left the house."

Eden squints at him, and then her face relaxes. "Oh, at Senator Little's. Everyone knows Miss Tunney works for him sometimes, and that's the only place she'd be at on the beach."

He objects. "She could've been at one of the restaurants!"

"Not on a Sunday night. So the Littles are involved. Hmm." Her eyes fly open. "He's her father! OMG!" She jumps halfway out her seat as she picks up her phone from the table. "I have to tell Sarah."

I reach out and grab her arm. "Stop, Eden. You can't. His family doesn't know, and the police are still, apparently, investigating. I shouldn't have said anything."

"I agree," Aiden says with a bit of a snarl. "We are trying to do this without messing more lives up." He turns to Eden. "Promise me you'll say nothing, okay?"

"Okay. For now." She picks up a chip, acting nonchalant. "So, are you getting any closer to finding the murderer?"

He holds his last bite of sandwich and nods. "I think we are. Detective Johnson is up at a couple of the colleges in South Georgia today. Several of the male students up there have histories of sexual assault and battery."

"But I asked and she wasn't assaulted sexually or beaten," I say.

He shrugs again. "Maybe he was interrupted. These things don't always make a lot of sense." He pops the last bite of sandwich into his mouth and crumples up his wrapper and napkin. "I have to get back to work."

They finish cleaning up the table, and I'm alone in only a few minutes. Maybe the police are right. Leslie was 'happy as a lark,' according to Miss Tunney. Maybe being in the Littles' home made her decide to wait for such an uncomfortable revelation. Maybe she wanted to go have a drink and forget it all. Nothing about her says she was predictable or responsible. Being part of the Little family probably felt overwhelming, and so she escaped to the party down at the beach. Maybe she really was just at the wrong place at the wrong time.

But, you know, that just doesn't feel right.

As I hang my new dress up in the bedroom closet, my phone chimes for a text. It's laying across the room on the table by the window, so I ignore it while I pull out shorts and a shirt and get dressed. All the while my phone keeps chiming. Finally I can't resist.

Four texts from Annie progress from "What are you doing?" to "I need you now."

I text back a trio of question marks and carry my phone into the bathroom where I put my hair up in a ponytail. It's too hot to work outside, so I'm going to start going through things in the downstairs junk room. I'm cleaning it out so that Eden can actually get in there and check out the furniture.

When my phone rings, I know it's Annie before I look at it.

"Hey. So you got my texts? Where are you? Who are you with?"

"I'm home, and I'm the only one here."

"Perfect! Uh…" She keeps talking but not at a volume that I can hear.

"Annie? What's going on?"

"I need you to come out to my house. Now. Eustis showed up here and wants to talk to us."

"Eustis is back? Where's she been?"

Annie blows out an exasperated breath. "She wants to talk to you. Says you aren't from here and can see things with fresh eyes. Plus, for some reason, she thinks you're a counselor or something? I told her you're just a normal person like us, but she insists." Annie pauses. "Wait. You're not a counselor or psychiatrist, are you?"

"No. Where would she get that idea?"

"It's Eustis. She's crazy. And you get nowhere arguing with her. Can you come out now?"

"Sure, I guess." So much for getting any work done today.

"Just a minute," Annie says, then proceeds to talk to Eustis, I assume.

"She says she needs something sweet. I'm trying to diet, and the only sweet thing I have here is Popsicles for the kids. Can you bring some cookies or something?"

"Sure." I know she can't see me rolling my eyes, but I try to convey it in my voice. "See you soon."

I don't have any sweets downstairs either except my piece of coconut cake, but I am not giving it to that crazy woman. Then I remember she's burying her daughter this week. "Okay, I'll take her something nice. But not my piece of coconut cake." I change into a nice pair of white shorts and a button-up, sleeveless shirt made of light blue linen, another recent purchase, this time from one of the downtown shops. The buttons are made of shell, and a small ruffle around the collar adds a touch of whimsy.

I jog down the stairs with a smile. I've decided to stop in Karen's Bakery and take Eustis something really nice that she can share.

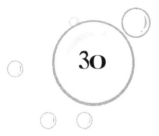

30

Living in a downtown area is nothing I've ever aspired to, but I'm finding that I love it. Even when I'm in my car, it's wonderful to visit the same small shops on a weekly basis, sometimes even more often, and this particular downtown being part of a small town means the same people tend to be in those businesses when I visit.

Karen's is a popular bakery that I visit more than I want to. Sometimes I find myself dropping by just to smell and look at the sweets case. However, I take every opportunity to stop and purchase, like today. If Eustis wants sweets, then she's getting the best.

"Jewel! Happy Friday!" Karen calls when I open the door.

The tall man she's waiting on turns and smiles. "Hello again, Mrs. Mantelle." Benjamin Perkins has his credit card in one hand but stretches out the other to me, and we shake.

The young lawyer's tie is still in the tight knot I watched him tie this morning, but he's in his shirtsleeves with no suit coat. "Hello," I say. "What is it they say about great minds thinking alike?"

He laughs as he hands Karen his card. "I've learned an assortment of treats from Karen's on the weekend helps keep a pregnant wife happy."

"Wise man. It was so nice to visit you and Amelia this morning. You have a lovely home and a lovely wife. I'm buying for someone not nearly as lovely or nice, but a trip to Karen's makes everything better!"

He moves his beribboned box down the counter. "Here, let me get out of your way. I'm sure your thoughtfulness will help." We both look into the glass cases in front of us. "It's hard to be angry when offered anything in here."

"True. But she's not really angry, more sad. She's had a horrible week and has been avoiding people."

Karen hands Benjamin his receipt and a

pen. "Oh, I'm sorry to hear that. Any idea what her favorite flavor might be? Or favorite dessert?"

"No, I don't really know her well, but I don't think she's picky. She's not very fancy. Maybe just an assortment of cookies? She seems like a coffee person, and cookies always go well with coffee. Plus, she could take them home or wherever she's headed to next; that's kind of unpredictable." Then I remember. "Oh! Annie loves your lemon bars. Do you have any of those? She says she's dieting, so maybe just one. She's had a rough week too."

"Absolutely. Do you want them in the same box?"

"Sure. I'm headed straight to Annie's now." I groan. "And her two grandkids will be there after school, so I guess add a couple more cookies."

Benjamin, his box of goodies in hand, rolls his eyes. "Isn't that how it is in this place? Always one more person to make happy. I'm glad my box is tied up, or I'd be tempted to add a lemon bar myself." He starts toward the door. "Thanks very much, Karen, and nice to see you again, Mrs. Mantelle. Hope your treats make everyone feel better."

He leaves, and Karen looks after him for

a moment, then shrugs. As she chooses a ribbon to tie up my box she asks, "You say you saw Miss Amelia this morning?"

"Yes, Lucy Fellows and I stopped by their home. Why?"

Karen could be cast as a loving, sweet grandmother in any Christmas commercial. Her gray hair is short but full of waves and she's a bit heavy, but most noticeable is the way that she just exudes happiness. This makes her full-faced frown noteworthy. "I don't know," she says. "Mr. Benjamin seemed worried. He worships our Amelia and has been over the moon since they found out about the baby."

"Oh, I didn't notice anything, but then again, I don't know them well. My daughter's husband became an absolute basket case the closer she got to delivery. Maybe that's all it is. She seemed perfectly healthy this morning."

"I'm sure. He also has a big job that will get even bigger if what I hear about him running for office is true." Karen winces. "Oh my, here I am gossiping. Don't listen to a word I say."

I pay and lift my box with two hands. "I know everyone will love all of this. Thank you." At the door, I turn back when she calls my name.

"Remember the first time we met? The advice I gave you?" She's grinning from ear to ear.

"How could I forget? You followed me outside and practically shouted it at me. 'Don't give up on happiness.'" Smiling at her, I ask, "Why?"

Karen leans her forearms on the glass-topped display case and nods at me. "I just like when folks follow my advice and it shows! Keep it up." She waves at me and turns to talk to a couple of women sitting at one of her small café tables.

I leave and head to my car.

Oh yes, I love living on Sophia Island.

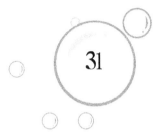

31

"'Bout time you got here." Eustis hits me with this charming greeting before I can get fully in the front door.

Annie throws up her hands. "Leave my friend alone. She didn't have to come at all. Look, she even went by Karen's." Annie takes the box out of my hands. "Here, let's get some sugar in the old witch to see if it makes her any sweeter."

I bend to rub Oscar's ears and take a breath. "Wow. Things seem kind of intense here. Good to see you again, Eustis. Sorry I'm late." I tried to imbue my apology with sarcasm, but I think they are both beyond noticing my weak attempt. They are in full-on abuse mode. Poor Oscar, being in the middle of all this.

Annie takes the box to the dining room table and opens it. "Look at all this. And you even got me a lemon bar." She lifts that out and carries it with her into the kitchen. "I'll get us some plates. I'm not taking a chance that Eustis will get this. I made coffee." She yells, "You want a cup?"

"I'm right here," I say. Oscar and I had followed her into the kitchen. "I'll fix my coffee." Then I whisper, "What's up?"

Annie whispers back. "She showed up here about an hour ago. Started rambling about how she saw *him* and that she had to get out of town and think. Now she's trying to figure out what to do next and wanted to talk to you for some crazy reason. All that counselor stuff and you not being from here, you know. I did get out of her that she knows you're not a real counselor, but she said you seemed real calm and professional." Annie raises her eyebrows. "I think it's just that you're the only person not on TV she's ever heard that doesn't talk Southern."

We both laugh, and taking our coffee and plates, we go back into the dining room, where Eustis is settled at the table like a child waiting for supper. She even has her hands in her lap.

She looks up at us. "I apologize. I've got to calm down so I can talk to you, Miss Jewel, but we have to hurry. I can't be here when the kids get here."

After letting Oscar outside with his own treat, Annie joins us at the table, with me at the end of the table and them on either side. Annie slices into her lemon bar with her fork. "She's insisting she won't stay long enough to see Markie and Leah, so I asked Annabelle to pick the kids up from school."

"Don't want to see them today." Eustis sadly shakes her head as she chooses a cookie for her plate. "Not today. I'll be too sad." She breaks off a piece of cookie, dunks it in her milky coffee, and takes a bite. When she finishes chewing, she lays the cookie down and looks up at me. "I'm just going to tell you what I've been thinking. Me and Leslie decided we'd never speak about it, but I'm beginning to believe it's what got her killed." She clears her throat, then says in a flat voice, "Leslie was raped on the beach the summer she turned sixteen."

Annie and I gasp, but before we can ask anything, Eustis holds up her shaking hand. "No. Let me get it all out. She was there with some friends. They were finally able to drive themselves to the beach, and they were there most every day. But they weren't allowed to stay after dark." She grimaces. "But you know how teenagers are. They know best." She dunks a piece of her cookie, waits for it to soak, and then pops it in her mouth before she continues. "I sent Mark to look for her. He'd also tried to warn her the beach at night wasn't no place for a girl. She was sweet as the day is long. Innocent as a baby." Tears fill her eyes, but she clears her throat again and blinks. Shaking herself, she sits up straighter. "He brought her home, told me she'd been just sitting under one of the picnic pavilions at Peele's Point when he pulled up. She wasn't even down at the party, so we thought it was all right…"

Annie says quietly, "But it wasn't."

"Nope. She got real quiet. Wouldn't talk or do much of anything. She'd always done a lot of drawing, but that became all she did the rest of that summer. I knew there was this one boy she'd been sweet on, so I figured he'd dumped her and she'd come around. I found one sketchpad just plumb full of this one boy's picture, so what else was I to think? I never was a real hands-on parent. Plus, she and her dad"—she scowls at us—"not her real dad, but my husband, well, they didn't get along, and he and I fought a lot. It was just a real hard time. Then when fall came, she wouldn't go to school. Just refused." She takes a bite of dry cookie and chews on that, staring down at the table.

Eustis sighs. "And I got tired of fighting her. I asked her if she was pregnant at one point in the middle of a fight, and the way she said she didn't think so, I knew she'd had sex." Slumping down in her chair now, she's almost mumbling. "So I fussed on her about that. Was that why she didn't want to go to school? Because the boy was there? She said no, but I didn't believe hardly anything she said at that point. By then she was drinking and running around with different friends, and the next thing I knew she was living over on the island." She shrugs and just sits there.

Annie motions with her eyes for me to say something, so I ask, "Um, when did you find out she'd been raped?"

"This is the part I really regret."

Annie and I can't help but look at each other with wide eyes when she says that, but we quickly shut down our judgment. I've got to admit, it's hard to do.

"I called her some names you call people, well, women who sleep around. It was in the middle of another fight, but…" Eustis looks like she could throw up. She swallows a couple times, then continues. "She yelled back that she wasn't a slut, she was raped."

It's so quiet in the house. Annie and I look stunned, and I know I can't help thinking about having my daughter tell me that. How helpless and angry I'd feel.

Then Eustis breaks the quiet. "It all came together. All those drawings of that boy. I found that sketchpad, where she'd been drawing so much back in the summer. She'd run off again, but I took it around to some of her old friends and they said he looked familiar, but he wasn't from around here. I even went to the police, but without Leslie, what could they do? Besides, by that point, they'd had quite a bit of contact with my out-of-control daughter and weren't likely to believe her anyways."

Annie looks at the clock on the wall. "Eustis, I hate to say it, but we've only got about ten more minutes before the kids get home. Why do you think this had anything to do with her being killed?"

Eustis's chin juts out. "I saw him. The day of my press conference. He was at the back with the police and the other officials."

Annie chokes on her coffee. "He's a police officer?"

"I don't know. I don't think so. He wasn't in a uniform or nothing. He was just standing back there. I couldn't figure out why he looked familiar, and then after it was all over, it hit me. But he was already gone. That's why I went into hiding. I tried to find that old sketchbook, but it's gone."

"This all seems pretty uncertain," I say. "What do you want us to do?"

"I've got to find him. Maybe I'll go find some of those kids that were on the beach that night. I've tried drawing his picture, but I'm not good at that. Guess Leslie got that from her father. I hear y'all talked to the senator?"

We nod. She nods back at us, then stands. "I've got to get out of here. It's just a shame. Old Stanford Little did more for our daughter in the last months of her life than I did the whole rest of it. Leslie had known he was her father for a while. I guess she finally decided to talk to him." Eustis slogs to the front door like she's walking through a swamp.

We get up and follow her. "Where are you going? Do you need anything?" I ask, but she shakes her head.

She keeps talking as she walks the length

of the porch to the driveway. "No, I'm staying at an old hunting cabin up in Georgia that doesn't get used until deer season. Belongs to someone in my husband's family." She turns at the end of the porch. "But don't go tellin' anyone. I'm still thinking on what to do. You can tell Willie at the funeral home to do something simple and I'll try to show up. If I don't, it's no different than my poor girl's life. She never could count on her momma." With a sad shake of her head, she turns and gets in the old, rusted-out car she apparently arrived in. It starts loudly, and then she turns it around to drive down Annie's long, sandy driveway.

We're quiet as we close the front door and move back to the table. We refresh our cups of coffee and make small talk about nothing while Annie gets out cups and the container of milk for the kids. Back at the table we sit, but we've run out of words. When Annie's phone rings it scares us both, and we jump.

"Annabelle," Annie says, looking at the screen with a scowl. "She better not be calling to say she forgot to get the kids. Annabelle? Where are you? Did you—"

She gasps and claps her hand over her mouth. Still listening she runs to lock the front door while yelling at me to lock the back door. I do, heart hammering, and then Annie grabs my arm and pulls me down the hallway. She's panting and I'm asking, "What's going on?" She pushes us into the hall bathroom, closes the toilet seat, then points at me to sit on it. She lets down the blue curtains on the small window and jerks them closed, and then she sits on the side of the bathtub. She says into the phone, "We're in the hall bathroom. Tell Aiden to hurry!" She doesn't hang up the phone, but lays it on the counter beside the sink. Then she puts her hand on my thigh.

"Jewel, Eustis is dead! Dead in her car in my driveway. Shot in the head right out there!" she screeches. Then she lowers her voice and closes her eyes, a death grip on my thigh. She prays, "Lord, let the police get here fast!"

And that's when Oscar starts barking his head off.

32

My heart is beating so hard that I can't hear anything outside this bathroom, especially over the barking. If the shooter was right out in the hallway, I would have no idea. Annie is crying but making no sound. I think I'm in shock because I can't process anything that is happening.

Until I hear the sirens.

Then there are shouts outside, shouts of Annie's name and mine. Of course, there's one policeman calling, "Momma," and that brings out a weak smile from both of us.

"I'm not sure my legs are steady enough to hold me," Annie says as she stands up. She peeks through the blue curtain. "There's

Aiden. He's motioning that it's okay for us to come out."

We rush to the front door, albeit on shaky legs. Oscar is first in the door, followed closely by Aiden, who hugs us both and leads us to the dining room table. "Officer Greyson is on his way right now to interview you two. There's not much to go on up at the crime scene. Looks like the shooter was waiting on Mrs. Callahan. Right at the end of the drive where she stopped to look before pulling out, looks like he, or she, stepped out of the woods, up to her window, and shot her from only a couple feet away."

Annie moans. "The kids didn't see her, did they?"

"No, Annabelle tried to turn into the driveway, but it was blocked by Miss Eustis's car. Then she saw, well, you know. She immediately pulled back out on the highway and called 911." He looks up as the front door opens. "Hey, Charlie," he says, then finishes answering his mother. "So the kids know, but they didn't see her. Annabelle took them to Amber's office."

Charlie Greyson sits down at the table beside me, which puts him across from Aiden. Annie is seated at the head of the table where I'd sat earlier. It was less than an hour ago that Eustis was sitting right where Aiden is. I find myself staring at the chair, but then wanting to look anywhere but there.

Greyson acknowledges us both with a nod. "Okay, ladies. We have approximately thirty minutes before Detective Johnson gets here from harassing those college guys up in Georgia. He was determined to pin Miss Callahan's murder on one of them, but obviously that's not the case. So let's not play around. Tell me what Eustis came out of hiding to tell you."

Annie takes a deep breath. "Okay. I'll start, but first hand me one of those cookies. To hell with my diet. I could've died today."

We told them everything, and I was given permission to go home. Detective Johnson had been delayed when a protest broke out at one of the campuses. He'd been badgering the wrong fraternity apparently. Lots of powerful alums.

Officer Greyson and I walk out together. I know the killer is gone, but it still feels safer to have Greyson near.

"Of course we knew where she was hiding out. It's not like half of the force hadn't hunted with Mark Callahan over the years." Officer Greyson steps away from the car when I open my door to get in. "But she wasn't under investigation. We figured she was just grieving in private. She always was an odd duck. She should've told someone what she'd seen."

I nod, then shrug. "But she was scared. Any ideas on who Leslie's rapist was? Are there any pictures or footage of the crowd at her news conference?"

"We're checking on that, but no one remembers anything like that. It wasn't that big of a deal that someone would've been making notes of the folks there." He pulls the door open wider. "Like I said, Officer Bryant has checked your house and I'll have a car out front tonight, but we don't think you're in any danger. If they'd wanted to get rid of you and Annie, well, there was ample opportunity."

I shudder and practically melt into my car seat. "Thanks. I'd almost managed to forget that."

He squints at me. "Sorry."

As I tug on the door he closes it, steps back, and waves. It's almost dark, and when I move into the woods enclosing the driveway, it gets even darker. They've created another path to the side to go around the crime scene, and I get by it without looking at the car.

Eden and Sarah are waiting at home. I'm glad they'll be there tonight, but right now I want something fast to eat and a few moments alone. My brain feels like it's taking a ride on a Tilt-a-Whirl.

At McDonald's I get a cheeseburger, fries, and a Coke, and then I head for the beach. At Main Beach there's a row of parking spaces that gives a straight-on view of the waves. I'm hoping it's late enough for the dinner rush for the beachfront restaurants to be over so that I can find an empty spot.

It is, and as I pull into a primo spot, the one at the end so there's only a car on one side of me, I roll down my windows to let the sound of the waves in. My cheeseburger and fries are heavenly. I gobble them down too fast at first, but then halfway through I realize I'm full, so I crumple everything up and put it in the bag. I step out of the car and take a seat on one of the benches looking out over the water.

I look up and down the beach and think of the fake turtle nest and the fact that a young woman lost her life near here. Then, in the other direction, there's the partying area where Eustis assumes her daughter was raped. Nearly ten years lie between those two things. What happened to Leslie in that span of time? Eustis said they hadn't discussed the rape, but did Leslie really tell no one? Not even Sarah? It has to be the impetus for her murder. But how, and why now? And why would her mother have to die too?

Relaxing and closing my eyes, I let the wind and the roll of the waves calm my spirit and my thoughts. Then I stand. "Time to go home and put this day behind me."

Fortified by fast food, I park and make my way up the front steps of my well-lit house. When the front door gives way to my shoving, I'm greeted by Eden, Sarah, Tamela, and Lucy. They offer me wine and food and any other comfort they can think of. In exchange, they want the whole story.

Once again I tell it all. They ask their questions, and I answer them the best I can. Sarah is shocked and upset to hear of Leslie's rape, and she excuses herself to go upstairs to bed. Leslie being so alone makes us all sad, and we're quiet after Sarah leaves the room.

There are more questions, and I describe Annie's and my race through the house to close ourselves in the bathroom with the tiniest window. As scary as the experience was, I find myself laughing. It's the exhaustion and the wine, but it still feels good to laugh, good and yet sad, so when the laughter fades, I finally push up from my comfortable lounge chair. "I have to go to bed."

We make our way to the front porch, where the police car at the end of the driveway reminds us of Eustis and Leslie. But as Tamela and Lucy say goodbye and leave, a wave from the policeman at the wheel does make me smile. After checking on Sarah and finding her asleep, Eden insists on cleaning up. She shoos me upstairs, so I climb up them, crawl into bed, and fall immediately into a hard sleep.

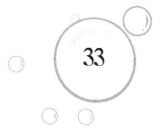

33

Rain wakes me while it is still dark. We'd had a good run of beautiful days, and to be honest a little bad weather feels good to me. I snuggle deeper into the covers and listen to the far-off thunder and watch the windows gleam softly with the distant lightning. The human impulse to be outside enjoying nice days apparently maintains its strength even when the nice days never seem to end, but that can get exhausting. It'll be good to stay home, inside, today. That thought is immediately followed by an unpleasant one.

There's a murderer out there.

Leslie's death meant that a murder had happened, but it could've been an accident. An act of passion or rage. At least I must've been telling myself that because Eustis being stalked and shot has brought me to a new level of fear. Someone obviously followed her from the hunting cabin to Annie's, then waited for her to leave. But why didn't they just shoot her at her hunting cabin? How long would it have been before she was discovered? They knew to hide Leslie's body, but they didn't think about that with Eustis?

Wait. What if it's two different people? Suddenly I'm out of the covers and sitting up on the edge of the bed. If someone saw what happened to Leslie on the beach, they could be protecting her killer because they think Eustis knew. But how would Eustis know anything? What did Eustis know that she had to be killed for? The rape? But that was so long ago and the rapist wasn't from around here.

Eustis would know that Stanford Little was Leslie's father. Maybe he changed his mind about introducing her as his daughter. Maybe Leslie did something to make him change his mind and then wanted to blackmail him. But why would he have told us after the fact that he was Leslie's father? There was no need to kill Eustis to protect that secret. I flop backward and lie flat, staring at the ceiling cracks. My thoughts are so scrambled that I'm not sure I'm actually awake. Maybe I'm dreaming.

I curl around my pillow and pull the covers back up. At this point my dreams might make more sense than my thoughts.

"Those final two hours of sleep were awful," I say to Eden. "It would've been better if I'd gotten up at five and started cleaning."

She's sitting at the kitchen table, coffee cup resting on her knees, which are pulled up to chin level in her chair. "Started cleaning what?"

"Anything." I'm standing at the sink and ask without turning around, "What if there were two murderers? One protecting the other?"

"Honestly? You're starting on this already?" She unfolds her legs and stands. "I can't think about this for one more moment. I have to get to work, and we have so much to get done here." As she walks past me, she gives me a one-armed side hug. "Sorry, but between you and Aiden, I've met my threshold for murder talk."

"Okay. Sorry."

She climbs the stairs and then from near the top yells, "Now that's an idea. Call Aiden. Y'all can talk each other out!" She laughs and then says hello to Sarah before she closes her door.

I hear Sarah running down the stairs.

"Good morning!" I say, cheerfully determined to not talk to at least one girl in my household about death and darkness.

Sarah comes around the corner wearing a pair of bright pink overall shorts and a purple bandeau top underneath it. Her hair is back in a braid, and she has on flip-flops. "Off to my art group." She reaches into the refrigerator and pulls out a bottle of water. "I talked to my folks last night. They were so sorry to hear about Leslie's mother, but it also made them want me to come home even sooner."

"I can understand that, but the police think we're perfectly safe."

She leans against the counter as she opens the water. "That's what I told them, but I'm flying home Tuesday, right after my final. They also wanted to send you some payment for letting me live here."

"Oh, nonsense. It's been a delight."

She smiles, but then her face clouds. "I know I might miss Leslie's funeral, but my folks are pretty adamant about me coming home." After a pause she says, "Can I ask you a question?"

"Sure." I turn in my chair to more fully face her.

"Did you take those pages out of my sketchpad, the ones Leslie did? They're missing, and you mentioned getting the one of me framed."

"No. I would never have done that without your permission. Maybe the police had to take them for evidence?"

She shakes her head. "I asked. They said no. Even had Aiden ask around."

I walk over to her and pat her back as I also lean against the counter. "Were they there when you got the book back from the police?"

She tips her head up just enough for me to see her eyes. "I don't know. I was having a bad day the day I picked it up. I didn't look until yesterday."

"I'll keep an eye out. I bet they'll turn up."

She brightens and smiles at me as she crosses the kitchen. Before she gets to the front door, Eden comes barreling down the stairs, calling out to her, "Give me a ride to work?"

They leave chattering, and I'm struck with a pang of missing my kids. Those hectic days of comings and goings, laughing and chattering, feel like yesterday sometimes, and then other times they are as untouchable and vague as my dreams from last night.

Maybe I should take Eden's advice and call Aiden to talk it all over with him. But why would a police officer want to discuss theories with a civilian, much less one that's friends with his mother? That's when it hits me. I actually hit my forehead with the heel of my palm and say, "D'oh! I'm part of a detective group. They'll talk to me about it!"

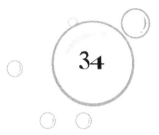

34

"It's a false crawl," Lucy explains to the handful of us standing around her. "For whatever reason the mama turtle decided not to make a nest. She crawled all the way up here, then crawled back in the water to lay her eggs somewhere else."

Before I could call my friends, Tamela had called me saying they'd found a false crawl if I wanted to come see it. I wasn't sure what a false crawl was, but if it would get me near my friends to discuss my two-killers theory, I was interested.

Lucy was already at the beach for a "peace talk" arranged by Benjamin Perkins for her and Sheila Hornsby. It appears he's done his job as Sheila is actually nodding along with

Lucy's explanation and Lucy is smiling in her adversary's direction every so often.

Tamela also called Annie, who was happy to bring Markie and Leah to the beach to run around, so they beat me here.

Cherry had come straight from her shift at the hospital and is yawning despite her interest in the tracks. "So this is why you kept saying that morning of the fake nest that there were no tracks."

Lucy smiles, but shifts her eyes to her right as if to remind Cherry that Sheila, the woman most sure the fake nest was real, is also standing there. Benjamin is playing peacemaker, but also future politician, as he brought a newspaper reporter along. The reporter's presence seems to have a big influence on Lucy and Sheila's good behavior, and it's kind of funny to watch.

"Let's step away from the chatter for a moment," Benjamin says to Lucy, Sheila, and the young reporter. "We want to make sure the facts about the joining of the sea turtle groups under one banner are correctly reported. We also want to get some pictures for the paper."

Lucy turns to us and rolls her eyes, but steps to the side and fluffs her hair with her fingers, although the brisk wind is doing plenty of fluffing on its own.

The rain left a pebbly texture all over the sand, but there is no sign of rain this morning. The remnants of the clouds provide sun cover and a beautiful backdrop for the reporter's pictures. Benjamin isn't wearing his normal suit, but still has on a starched shirt and khakis. His dark hair looks as styled as ever, and he's freshly shaved.

I'm alone in watching the photo session. Tamela is walking near the water, and Cherry said goodbye with a barely disguised yawn before heading over the dunes to her car. Annie is keeping the kids out of the water, or at least pretending to. She's yelling something at them, but I can't hear her over the surf. Their shorts look pretty wet from way up here, and I laugh, thinking of bringing Carver to the beach. I stand with my back to the dunes, watching everyone and counting my blessings.

A gust of wind blows, and Lucy, Sheila, and Benjamin each get a face full of sand. I turn away from the wind and watch as they break apart, shielding their faces and laughing. As they come back together, Benjamin's hair flops onto his forehead. Hair gel doesn't stand a chance against sea breezes. That's when it hits me.

That same jolt of fear from last night stabs my chest. I've seen Benjamin before—in Leslie's sketches. All those young people, and the one she drew from memory. A horrible memory.

No. That wasn't him. He's not even from here, I argue in my head. He wasn't here then; he said he didn't come here until Amelia brought him in college. But wait—then how did he know about my house? That morning at the breakfast place he said he'd seen Craig's aunt Corabelle in the window. That was at least ten years ago.

He lied. He lied about never being here before.

And he was at the Littles' house on Sunday night. He didn't go in the house with Amelia because he stayed outside putting up the garden hose. Leslie was in the kitchen, but then she went outside—where he was! Of course she would've recognized him. She'd been drawing him for ten years.

Then I think of Eustis with a queasy, sinking feeling. He knew where to find her because of what I said at Karen's Bakery, I bet. He knew I was going to Annie's and taking cookies to a crazy old lady who had had a very bad week. Oh no. I led him right to her. I close my eyes and try to breathe, and another piece falls in place. She saw him at the press conference. He's a lawyer, so it would make perfect sense for him to be at the courthouse compound.

I turn to the side as the horror washes over me. I have to act cool, so I take a deep breath, but as I turn back toward them to look again, he is there. A foot away from me.

Benjamin says loudly, "You look a little tired. Let me walk you to the bench." Then he tells the reporter over his shoulder, "Sheila and Lucy are the stars. Get some pictures of them closer to the water." He wraps his arm tightly around mine, and then I feel it. "Yes," he whispers. "That's my gun. You saw what it did yesterday. Let's not have a repeat. We're going to keep walking through the parking lot. My car is just across the street."

"I'm not…" I try to stop walking, but he's walking quickly and he drags me along behind him, practically lifting me off my feet.

"If I have to shoot you here, I will. And then I'll shoot whoever is following us."

I try to alert my friends, but the wind and waves are so loud. I'm not sure they can even see us so close to the parking lot the way the beach slopes.

He jabs the barrel of the gun into my ribs. "Why can't you people just leave me alone? It's been a nightmare since the moment I saw her come waltzing out of my father-in-law's house. What in the world was she doing there?" His voice strains with tension and his grip on me tightens. "I couldn't let her go back inside to tell everyone, so I didn't. We were just kids, but no one would understand that now, would they? Not with all the 'Me Too' stuff these days. I have a lot of plans, and we have a baby coming. She wanted to get even. I could tell from the way she looked at me."

The parking lot is full of cars, but no people are around. This is happening so fast that I can't think. Where is everybody?

He shakes his head with a dark laugh. "Then talk about being in the wrong place at the wrong time. I'm just doing my job, walking out of the jail after a meeting, and I stop for two seconds. Two seconds! I take a look at what's going on with the news cameras, and that woman stares at me like she knows me. It didn't take long to find out who she was. I couldn't figure out how she knew me, but then I was at the police station and saw myself in that sketchpad. Guess that tramp was some kind of artist. What a joke!" At the street, we have to stop to let a couple cars go by. In his other hand Benjamin clicks his key fob, and I see the headlights on a light gray car flash just across the street. We are almost there. But I am not getting in that car.

I preached to my kids, especially to my girls, about never getting into a car with someone who wanted to hurt them. Better to be in public with a gunshot wound than alone, dumped on the side of the road to die.

How easy that was to say. And how hard it is to do.

I'm not sure I can pull away from him. He's strong, but even a strong man has a hard time carrying a grown woman with one arm, and now he's lost some momentum as we wait for traffic. In the middle of the street I purposely drop from my feet and fall. I find my voice and scream, "Help! He has a gun!" as loud as I can. Benjamin Perkins struggles with me for a moment, but I'm kicking and screaming, bystanders are turning around, and his car is right there. Luckily, he decides escape is his best bet. He lets go of me and runs to his car.

My legs are jelly, but I know he won't hesitate to back over me, so I roll and crawl to the closest parked car, then roll under its back bumper. Benjamin screeches off, and I lay my cheek down on the pavement, waiting for someone to come tell me I'm safe.

Who knew warm pavement could feel so good?

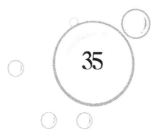

35

Cherry had been pulling out of the parking lot and saw the whole thing. She reached me and, after making sure I wasn't hurt, helped me take a seat in her car.

"Someone called 911, right?" I ask. "Told them to stop him?"

"Yes. There's Lucy and Tamela." Cherry rolls down her window and waves them over.

"What happened?" Lucy demands through the window as Tamela runs to my side of the car.

"It was Benjamin Perkins. Get in the back seat. The police will be here soon."

They get in and lean as close as they can toward the front seat. Lucy asks, "What did Benjamin do?"

"He raped Leslie ten years ago. Then killed both her and her mother to hide it." I take another sip of water from the bottle Cherry dug out of her work bag. "I recognized him from a drawing of Leslie's and couldn't hide my shock."

Cherry is grim. She reaches over and rubs my arm. "He had a gun on Jewel and dragged her over here. She fell down and got away from him. Smart move." We all watch as a police car pulls up and Aiden jumps out.

He dashes over to Cherry's car and looks inside. "Where's Momma?"

Lucy points to the beach. "There with the kids. I don't think she knows anything is going on. Cherry texted me to come up here, but Annie was too far away to hear me yell. Plus, she has the kids."

"Go on. Check on her," Officer Greyson says as he joins us. "I'll take it from here."

"Have they caught him?" I ask through my open window.

"Yep. He knew he had to get off the island quick, but he wasn't quick enough. They caught him just as he crossed the bridge. The officer even saw him throw the gun into the water. They'll get to recovering that." He looks over his shoulder, then bends closer. "That's Detective Johnson's car; we are going to need to get your statement. If you suggest going to the station, it'll catch him off guard. You can have Mrs. Berry just drive you there, okay? It'll give you a minute to calm down."

I nod as I look at Cherry. "Is that okay? I know you are so tired."

She winks and smiles. "I'll never be that tired."

Lucy slams her back door. "I'm coming too."

Tamela sits back to put on her seat belt. "Somebody better text Annie. She'll kill us if she misses this."

We were at the police station for less than an hour. Detective Johnson wanted to interview me at first, but with the prospect of a double murderer coming in, he lost interest. He dismissed me, saying Officer Greyson could take my statement.

On the way home, with Annie squished into the back seat between Lucy and Tamela, Centre Street traffic picked up and we remembered how crowded downtown gets thanks to the Saturday farmers market.

Cherry pulls into a pleasant surprise of a parking place right at the entrance to the market. "I don't know about y'all, but I could do with a pastry. This guy here has the best."

We are all opening our car doors in response to this, and with orders to get whatever looks good, Cherry and Tamela head into the crowds between the stalls. Lucy, Annie, and I claim a spot big enough for all of us on the wall outside the Methodist church.

"Detective Johnson didn't know whether to scratch his watch or wind his butt, did he?" Annie says from her seat down the wall. "That's one of my favorite lines from *Steel Magnolias*," she adds with a wink.

"Thank goodness," I say. "I just hope Benjamin confesses and there isn't a trial."

Lucy gives me a squeeze. "I'm willing to bet Stanford Little will see to it there isn't a trial. He'll figure out some way to get a plea deal that keeps his family out of the news. I can't help but feel sorry for Amelia, pregnant and finding out her husband is a rapist and a murderer."

Puddles in the street splash whenever a car drives through them and the plants and trees still drip, but there are bits of sunshine coming through the cloudy sky. The air smells warm but fresh, and I take a deep breath. It's hard to imagine that earlier this morning I had a gun stuck in my side. My shudder is cut short by Cherry's announcement that they are back, bags in hand.

A peach turnover, a cherry pastry, a blueberry muffin, and a cinnamon roll all get spread out on the wall, laid on a line of napkins. We pinch and taste but mostly sit and stare at the normalcy all around us. People walk past us with their market purchases, some pushing bikes, many walking dogs or strollers. Everything looks so... so normal.

Lucy is standing in front of those of us that are seated, and she suddenly straightens. "Uh-oh. Look at that sky. Rain will be here soon."

I've learned rain here often comes suddenly and hard, so I join in the scurry of wrapping up our pastries and dashing to the car. We're not alone, as suddenly everyone is moving faster. A deep rumble of thunder causes those not hurrying to do so, including the merchants at the market who begin pulling their wares under their tents.

By the time we all pile into the car, we are laughing. We've just gotten in when the bottom drops out.

As the windows fog up on the inside and the rain streaks down the outside, the noise level makes talking virtually impossible. We sit, and as the laughter dies, we are quiet. It's been a full morning from standing on the beach just after daybreak.

When the rain lessens I say, "I feel kind of bad for laughing when so many people are going through such terrible things."

Cherry smiles sadly at me. "Being a nurse, I can tell you laughing is sometimes the only good response when bad things happen."

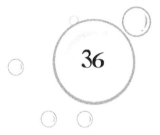

36

"Nice to meet you, Mrs. Benoit," Annie says to Sarah's mother. Mrs. Benoit flew in last night for the funeral—and probably to make sure her daughter gets on that plane to Texas this evening.

We're crowded into the large fellowship hall of Eustis's country church on Tuesday afternoon. The funeral for Leslie and her mother was held this morning in the big funeral home on the island, as it had been planned when it was only for Leslie. Though that remained the same, Eustis's church firmly insisted the reception be held here. It's a mild day with a bright, blue sky and fresh greenery everywhere. At first, the country church seemed like a long way to drive, but after such a sad funeral I found the trip very restful.

Annie shakes Sarah's mother's hand, then pats their grasp with her free one. "Your Sarah has been such a sweetheart through all this. We'll miss her."

Mrs. Benoit nods and then takes her hands from Annie's to put one arm around her daughter. "We've been so worried, and we will be glad to have her home." She turns to her daughter. "Let's go get something to eat." Without a look in our direction they move toward the front of the room.

"I guess I understand her not being very friendly," I say.

Annie lifts an eyebrow at me. "Go ahead. Say it. You know you want to."

I elbow her and look down as I work my mouth to keep from smiling. "Stop. It's a funeral."

"Okay, I'll say it: Bless her heart. Listen, though, I'm back on kid duty in a minute. Trying to help as much as I can." She shakes her head. "Poor Mark is hating all this attention, but he's acting right normal. I'm not sure how long he can keep it up."

I step over to the table full of plastic cups of ice tea. "He looks good in his suit. He and Amber seem to be getting along." I look for someone to ask if all of the tea is sweet, but I should know better by now. I choose a glass of water.

Annie crosses her arms and clicks her tongue at me as she picks up a cup of tea. "They're going to try again on that marriage of theirs. She and the kids are moving back out here tonight. All of them have had the stuffing knocked out of them. Plus, that girl of mine needs to lay low, wait and see if she's in trouble for the rooms at The Settlement."

We look around the busy hall as we sip our drinks. Lucy and Tamela wave to say they are coming our way. I finally met Lucy's friend, Davis, and he's as good-looking and polished as promised. He was at the funeral, but Lucy rode with Tamela and Cherry to the reception since he had to go back to work.

Lucy reaches us first and hugs Annie. "How is that sweet Eden? She was so upset at the funeral."

Annie shakes her head as she stretches to look around. "I saw that, but then I was busy with Markie and Leah and didn't get to talk to her or Aiden. I don't see them here, though."

"No," I say as Cherry joins our group. "They were going to go take a walk on the beach. She and Sarah are kicking themselves over not knowing what happened to Leslie. Apparently she never mentioned the rape, just like Eustis told us. Aiden and I tried explaining that it's just not easy to share something like that, especially when you're so young. Eden's mother got her an appointment with a counselor at the women's center tomorrow morning."

Cherry speaks up, "Are y'all going to eat? There's no line right now and I'm starving."

We fill our plates and find seats at the end of a long table, guided by Cherry away from the rest of the crowd. As she sits down she says, "Okay, Lucy, there's no one around. Tell us what Stanford had to say." Cherry rolls her dark eyes. "She wouldn't tell us in the car over here."

Stanford had refused to talk to anyone, even the police, until Monday. He said his first duty was to his pregnant daughter and his family. He met with Lucy last night, and we've all been waiting to hear what he had to say.

Annie huffs. "Good thing. We all want to know. Just be glad Annabelle took the kids back to my house so I can sit with y'all. I know she would've waited for me to be around, right?"

No one answers her assumption, but before she can frown and complain, we all turn our attention to Lucy.

She speaks softly but clearly. "Benjamin was here when he was in college, just that one trip. About that night at Stanford's house, well, they finally determined that only Benjamin had said he'd seen the girl in the pink dress heading down the beach toward Peele's Point. But he made it seem like it was common knowledge, like they'd all seen her. Of course they had no reason to doubt him. At the time it didn't really matter to anyone but Stanford"—she sighs and tears fill her eyes—"when all along the poor girl was already dead. She came out of the kitchen door, just like Tunney said, where Benjamin was rolling up the garden hose. Leslie recognized him, and he realized she recognized him like he told you, Jewel. Arrogant toad that he is, he told everything to the police. Explained his oh-so-reasonable actions. He tried to keep her quiet and ended up strangling her. He then hid her body on the side of the house in the bushes and went inside for dinner with the family." Lucy shudders. "He had plenty of time to decide what to do but knew he couldn't leave her at his father-in-law's, so in the middle of the night he drove back to Stanford's house to get her. He was pretty proud of his turtle nest idea. Apparently he actually thought he'd get away with claiming it was an accident he killed her or that she attacked him and he acted in self-defense. He was full of stories." Her voice trails off and she shakes her head. "He thought being Stanford Little's son-in-law would save him. Then he found out Stanford was Leslie's father."

Tamela draws in a quick breath. "So the senator told his family about Leslie?"

"Yes. That was another thing he wanted to do this past weekend. He paid for the funeral and is reimbursing the church for all this. Not that they asked, but he said they can do what they want with the money. He said he just couldn't come to the funeral. It would make an unnecessary scene." She finishes with a long sigh.

We're quiet, and no one is eating.

"How's Amelia?" Cherry asks.

"Okay. About as expected. She's left town, of course. Stanford too. He said talking to me was his last thing to do. He wanted to thank all of us. Especially you, Jewel."

Lucy pats my hand, and I nod at her.

Annie leans forward. "Aiden says the police are pretty red-faced about all this. Here the murderer was, waltzing in and out of the jail and courthouse, and they even had a sketch of him!" She widens her big, blue eyes. "Which he then stole right out from under their noses. Guess they dismissed the sketches as no more than doodles. No one will admit to actually looking at them."

Cherry smiles at me. "Thank goodness our Jewel recognized him. And thank goodness you didn't let him take you with him."

Tears spring to my eyes. "I'm so thankful for all of you. Craig offered to come home. I know you're all wondering, but I told him I'm okay with my friends." I get a side hug from Annie on my right and from Tamela on my left.

After a minute, our hunger and the smell of the home-cooked food pull us back to our plates. As our plates clear, so does the large fellowship hall. Sarah stops to say goodbye; her mother stands off to the side, watching but not meeting our eyes. Annie's extended family waves to her as they leave. Amber and Mark are still seated alone near the door. They look tired but have locked hands. Church members are cleaning up empty plates, and as they come to us, we give them our trash and our thanks.

"It's what we do," an older man says.

Only a few other people are still seated. Annie groans. "Guess it's time to head out."

The five of us begin to move and stand.

"You drove by yourself?" Tamela asks me.

"Yes. I wasn't sure if Eden needed a ride, and then she ended up not coming. It really was a beautiful drive." We chat as we leave the large, open room and stroll out into the sunshine. Only a few cars are left near the front of the lot.

Annie stops for a minute and looks at Mark and Amber, who are walking out of the building behind us. "Jewel, you mind giving me a ride home? Let those two have a bit of peace and quiet?"

"Sure," I say as she motions to her daughter that she'll be riding with me. We're all in shades of black and remind me of a flock of crows as we walk together.

As Annie and I open the doors of my car, Tamela rolls down her driver's-side window. "Jewel. I forgot to give you something." She holds out a folded piece of paper, and I step over to the car to take it.

"What is it?"

"Just something I think you'll like." Then she bends her head toward me and whispers, "Maybe don't mention it to Annie." She quickly pulls away.

"I heard that," Annie says as she flounces around the end of the car. "What is it?"

I finish unfolding the paper, and after I read the heading, I have to press my lips together to keep from smiling. I hold the paper away from my friend's reaching grasp and continue studying it as I head to my car door.

"What? Come on, Jewel, what is it?" she demands. "What is it I don't need to know? You think you have friends, and then they want to leave you out of stuff. I guess she thought I'd be busy with the kids today, didn't she?" She fusses the whole time we get into the car. I keep mum as I buckle my seat belt.

As she slams her door, she spouts, "Get that air conditioning going and tell me what that so-called friend of mine is leaving me out of this time."

She narrows her eyes at me when I finally hand the paper over. With a huff she looks at it and then says, "Oh…"

I burst out laughing. "What? You're not interested in an application to join the Turtle Trackers?"

Annie cuts her eyes at me. "I need new friends." Then she laughs and points at the windshield. "Now, take me back to our island."

CHECK OUT ALL OF KAY'S SOUTHERN FICTION
at
www.KayDewShostak.com
and she loves being friends
on Facebook with readers!

Don't miss book 1
in the Southern Beach
Mystery series!
The Manatee Did It

Book 3
The Shrimp Did It
is also coming soon!

CPSIA information can be obtained
at www.ICGtesting.com
Printed in the USA
LVHW021106260921
698747LV00001B/184